SHOPPING FOR A TURKEY

JULIA KENT

Editor: Elisa Reed

Cover design: Yocla Designs

Join my newsletter at http://www.jkentauthor.com/newsletter/

SHOPPING FOR A TURKEY

I don't understand Americans.

Or, as we say in Scotland, I dinna understand ye eedjits.

And I definitely dinna understand the crazy mother-in-law of my cousin Declan. Who in their right mind names a wee dog Chuffy?

I'm stuck in New York after ma agent makes a bloody mess of an otherwise good endorsement contract for a sports towel company, and this crazy American holiday–Thanksgiving–is in two days.

The invitation to spend it in Mendon, Massachusetts, with the Jacoby family is about as appealing as rotten haggis. As far as I can tell, Thanksgiving is about stuffing yerself silly, watching pathetic American "football," while fighting with relatives ye only see once a year.

If I wanted that last one, I'd head back to Scotland, where we dinna need a holiday to be salty to each other.

Ma firm answer is nae.

Until I remember Amy is part of the family.

Suddenly, I'm available.

Eager, even. Perhaps she'll pull ma wishbone. I hear that's part of the Turkey Day festivities, aye?

What I canna admit, though, is how she pulls ma heart-strings, too.

Which shouldna feel better than the wishbone, but it does.

And here comes Amy's mother with another holiday tradition, this one a bit early.

A sprig o' mistletoe, dangling right above Amy's bonnie head.

--

Shopping for a Turkey features Scottish football player Hamish McCormick and Amy Jacoby as they navigate unusual cultural norms, new traditions, and the undeniable attraction between these two characters, who have appeared as supporting players in Julia Kent's *New York Times*-bestselling *Shopping* series.

It's their turn to have their own all-new spinoff series. And to pull the wishbone. ;)

Listen to the audiobook, narrated by Shane East and Emma Wilder.

1

Hamish

"I'm sorry, Hamish, but the contract's broken with Towelz2Teamz. No photo shoot, no ad campaign, no media appearances."

My agent's voice has a cringing tone, as if he thinks I'll blow.

Might as well prove him right.

"WHAT? *Why?*" I scream into the useless glass screen of my mobile. I'm in a hotel room on the thirty-third floor in New York City after a three-day modeling shoot for a new kind of kinesiology tape, and check out is in forty minutes.

"Turns out the chief financial officer was embezzling from the company. Hid all the money in cryptocurrency. The Feds are sorting it out and T2T has decided to end all contracts."

"Yer kidding!"

"Nope. I never kid about money. You know that. You get to keep the kill fee, though."

"Kill fee?"

"They have to pay you if they cancel the contract."

"I get paid *not* to work?"

Jody chuckles softly. "Basically." His low voice drops a bit, as if I'm supposed to know this already.

"Then sign me up fer hundreds of these contracts and let 'em cancel!"

"It doesn't work that way."

"Dinna tell me it doesn't. They're canceling and I'm being paid."

"It's not the full amount of the contract."

"How much is it?"

He quotes a pathetic figure. Still, it's a figure I've done nothing to earn.

"That's bloody awful! And I'm stuck now."

"Stuck?"

"I'm here in New York. There's some stupid American holiday coming up. I'm in the airline app on ma phone and there's nothing. Nae seats on flights home."

"No seats at all, or no *cheap* seats? I do not understand your obsession with flying coach. For a guy your size, it's like human origami."

"If it's ma own money, I fly economy. And I even looked at business class. Three thousand dollars fer a seat! And that's just New York to London! If I'm spending three thousand on a seat, it better be a good shag and cook me breakfast in the mornin'."

"It's Thanksgiving weekend. Today is Tuesday. Everyone flies the Wednesday before. Good luck finding a seat in coach."

"I'm giving thanks to nae one fer this, Jody. Get me home."

"I can't. Book first class."

"The damn towel company should arrange fer ma ticket home to Scotland."

"They aren't required to."

"Damn it, Jody! I told ye–"

"Cool your jets, Hamish."

"I have nae jets! That's the problem! Get me on a jet across the pond to where I belong!"

"It's an expression. Means calm down."

"Why the hell would I be calm right now when I just got screwed?"

"Before you blow a gasket, I also have good news. There's another contract."

"Well, why in bloody hell didn't ye lead wi' that? Ye start with the good to soften the blow from the bad."

"It's not the greatest offer. I knew if I started with it, you'd reject it."

"But now that I have nae options, ye think I'm desperate enough to say yes to anything?"

Silence. I get nothing but silence from Jody.

My long sigh betrays me. "Jesus, ye know me well."

"Right. It's in Boston."

"*Nooooooo*! Why is all the work up there?"

"What's wrong with Boston? I thought you had relatives there."

"I do. They're all a bit crazy, though. Rich buggers, the lot of them. The minute ma uncle James learns I'm in town, he'll be using me as his wingman."

"What's wrong with that?"

"The guy's older than Solomon and thinks he's ma age."

"Well, that's the thing–the contract is *because* of James McCormick."

"What?"

"He reached out. Said his company is looking for a spokesman for some of their properties. Boston is such a sports town."

"Boston has nowt to do with football!"

Did ye know ye can hear a man choke on his coffee through a phone? Either that, or Jody swallowed his tie.

"Have you heard of a little football team called the Patriots, Hamish? Six-time Super Bowl champions?"

"That's nae football. That's a bunch of overpaid men in tights chasing a coohide turd."

"Stephon Gilmore earned $13 million last year, plus bonuses, for chasing a turd in tights."

"I'll be damned. Maybe I'm playing the wrong kind of football. But mine isna misnamed."

"Soccer, Hamish. It's called *soccer* here."

I make a sound.

It's not a polite one.

"I know damned well what it's called, but that doesna make it right. Just because ma gran called Da her baby doesna make him wee again."

"The negative attitude doesn't sell product, Hamish."

"I'm never selling American football, Jody."

"I'm not talking about endorsements. *You're* the product you're selling. Don't forget that."

"I thought I was selling ma football skills."

We both laugh heartily at that.

"Speaking of your skills, there's a nude photo shoot coming up for Peak Performance Magazine. You ready?"

"If by *ready*, ye mean have I plucked all the mutant escape hairs off ma body and done a bowel cleanse formulated with more precision than a chemical engineer uses at a pharmaceutical plant, then na."

"No?"

"The shoot's in two weeks. I'll do a shred and cleanse before then."

"Right. Makes sense. You'll stuff yourself silly at Thanksgiving, anyhow."

"Why?"

"*Why?*"

"Is there an echo, Jody?"

"People eat until they can't fit in their pants, Hamish."

"And then what? A post-prandial orgy?"

He sighs. "You really know nothing about our Thanksgiving?"

"Battle of Culloden."

"Huh?"

"What do ye know about the Battle of Culloden?"

"Uh, nothing."

"There ye go. Don't be smug with me for no' knowing about some day when ye all worship turkeys."

"That's not what Thanksgiving is about."

"What, then?"

"It's celebrating the settlement of the English colonies in America. We eat turkey, mashed potatoes, cranberry sauce, sweet potatoes, squash–"

"Ye go into the woods and find a big bird and kill it?"

"We buy them at the grocery store."

"That's no' as exciting."

He laughs. "Nothing's ever exciting enough for you, Hamish. You're an adrenaline junkie."

"That's just another term for footballer."

"Absolutely." A buzz in the background makes it clear he has a text on his other phone. Jody carries three. I half expect two are for wives he's hiding from each other, and the third is for work. "Gotta go."

"Right." I sigh. "Nae way home?"

"Charter a jet."

"Canna afford it."

"Then take the Boston contract."

"Fine. But James McCormick uses me as eye candy."

Another silence ensues.

"Eye candy?"

"Aye."

"Eye or aye?"

"Yer saying the same word, Jody."

"E-Y-E or A-Y-E candy?"

"E-Y-E. The other doesna make sense."

"Neither one makes sense. How does he use you as eye candy?" He begins to choke. "Is it–are you and he..?"

"DEAR GOD, nae!" I thunder out. "He's ma uncle! And he's ancient!"

"Right. Of course."

"Besides, he's no' ma type."

"You have a type when it comes to men?"

"Ha. Na. I like women. James is fine for an uncle, but he's a bit of a priggish braggart."

"Then how is he using you as eye candy? I thought you said he turned you into his wingman."

"Same thing. He brings me around fer attention. I do draw a crowd, ye know."

"You sure do, and I hope that continues forever. Your looks are moving the money needle in the right direction."

"But it all starts with ma footwork."

He coughs discreetly. "Of course."

"I think James brings me places so he gets attention."

"What's wrong with that?"

"Nae one likes to be used."

"Use him back. Take the contract."

A flash of Amy Jacoby, that sweet young firebrand who's the sister of my cousin's wife, makes Boston more appealing.

"Fine. I'll sign. Canna be worse than anythin' else I've done."

"I forgot to mention the hot dog costume." His voice makes it clear he's joking, but for the right price, I'll wear damn near anything.

"A sexy dog? I'm no' into fetish work, Jody. Ye know, even I have a line."

Jody's heavy sigh comes through loud and clear. "Good luck getting back to Scotland, Hamish. I'll let McCormick's people know it's a go."

The call ends and I go back to the airline app, running a

frustrated hand through my damp hair. Fresh out of the shower, I was packing up when Jody called. Now I have to check out, find something to do and a way to get to Boston, and be in limbo while Jody talks to James' people.

My stomach growls.

And I need lunch, too.

What I need more is a personal assistant.

Auburn hair a few shades darker than mine, attached to a snappy mouth and a fine, lush body, comes to mind.

I wonder what she's doing now?

Amy

It's the call no one ever wants to receive.

You know the one.

Where your father tells you your mother broke her leg while they were having wild sex?

Right. *That* one.

I'm at the gym, thirty minutes into a stair machine that's destroying my glutes, and it feels so good. Burning off nervous energy from turning in huge projects for my MBA has become a ritual.

Group projects are the worst. Half the people don't listen, everyone wants to be a visionary but not an implementor, and the posturing for status makes my teeth ache.

Cursed by an intuitive sense for optimization, I am usually left being visionary, implementor, and coffee deliverer.

And I can't help myself.

So here I am, at the gym at one in the afternoon, just after the lunch rush, working out my stress hormones, feeling them leak out of my pores in the form of sweat, when an innocent ring tone upends *everything*.

"Amy, honey, before you worry, your mother is just fine. We're at Metro Hospital. She's being taken into x-ray. They're pretty sure her leg's broken," Dad explains, sounding weirdly contrite.

"Dad? What? What happened? Broken? How?"

Silence. *Dead* silence. Creeping into my senses, my dad's hesitation makes my skin prickle.

"We had an unfortunate accident."

"Car accident?"

"No."

"You... tripped?"

"No."

"DAD!!"

"We were in bed."

"In bed? How did Mom break her leg in bed–*ohhhhhhhh*."

"It's–I don't want to get into it. But I need your help."

"Okay."

"I need you to call Marco Aleandro."

"The carpenter?"

"Yep."

"Why?"

"There's a problem with the ceiling beam in our bedroom."

"Wait. *Whew*. So, the beam fell on Mom while you were in bed sleeping?"

"Not quite."

I don't like the direction this conversation is taking.

"The beam cracked in half and fell on you two while you were watching television in bed?"

"Um... not quite that, either. And I need you to remove the swing before Marco arrives. The ceiling hook might have caused the problem."

"Swing? I thought you said you were in your bedroom.

What does the swing set in the back yard have to do with this?"

His pause feels like falling over a cliff into a black hole.

There's nothing you can do about it, it's endless, and you'll never be the same again, no matter where you end up.

"Um," he says, lowering his voice. "It's actually a sex swing."

"DAD!"

"The beam might be cracked, which is an expensive repair, and when we heard the creaking sound, your mother panicked and began twisting. Then I lost my footing and Marie pivoted and–" His voice cracks a little. "I didn't know a penis could bend like that and not snap clean off."

"ENOUGH!"

"Sorry, honey. But you asked."

They say couples start to take on each other's attributes over time. Mom is definitely rubbing off on Dad.

In more ways than one.

Excuse me while I go puke.

"Amy? I'm really sorry." Dad sounds mortified, his voice hoarse, the ends of words dropping off into sighs. "But before you call Marco, get the swing off the hook and put it in the closet. He'll let me know how bad the damage is. Plus, he's a sheetrock guy, and there's definitely some cracking in the ceiling. How close are you to home?"

"I'm at the gym." I grab my keys and water bottle off the machine I'm standing on. Thankfully, it's quiet here, and no one's super close to me. This is a conversation best kept private.

"At the gym? Good for you. You always were disciplined, kiddo."

Apparently, I *was* at the gym. I see how my afternoon is going to go.

Cleaning up my parents' messes.

"Great! Five minutes away. Could you do this... now?"

"Of course." I'm already halfway across the cardio floor, headed toward the glass double doors.

"And set up the pull-out couch."

"Huh?"

"Your mother broke her femur. She won't be able to use stairs for weeks. We'll have to create a makeshift bedroom for her in the living room."

"Poor Mom."

"Yeah," Dad says. "And can you let Shannon and Carol know? Just leave out the sex swing part."

"Oh, I promise. Last thing I want to do is talk about your sex life with my sisters."

His chuckle makes my stomach hurt.

"No one likes to think about their parents like... that."

"No one likes to be asked to move their parents' sex swing off a hook because they broke the house frame, Dad. You owe me for some therapy bills."

"Add it to our tab. I think we're up to the year 2076 for your sessions."

"Fifty-four years isn't enough."

A long pause comes next, stretching like emotional taffy, the hesitation clear even though I can't see Dad.

Then I realize what he's about to ask.

It's a big ask.

"Um, any chance you could stay with us at the house?"

"I am staying at the house, Dad."

"I mean, through the entire long holiday weekend? I know you have your place in Amherst, but I could use the help."

"It's okay, Dad. I'm here anyhow. No problem staying until Sunday."

Mumbling comes through on the phone, then Dad's rushed voice. "You're a doll. Gotta go. Thanks for handling this, honey."

I stare at the phone for a second and then open my texts, creating a new message between Shannon, Carol, and me.

How do you even begin to describe this?

The direct route is best.

Mom broke her leg while she and Dad were having kinky sex. They're at the hospital, I type and send.

Instantly, three dots appear. And then:

Mum and Da haven't had sex in years, ye silly fool. Quit joking, Shannon replies.

Or at least, I think it's Shannon.

What? I type back, staring dumbly at the reply.

The prank isna even guid, she answers. *Try better. Grease a guinea pig and put it under the sink where Mum keeps the cleaning supplies.*

Mum? Da? Why is Shannon writing so weirdly?

This isn't a joke! I type back. *Mom broke her leg while she was hanging from a sex swing in their bedroom. I now know way too much about how Dad's penis bends, too.*

Three dots appear. Oh, goody. What's next?

Now ye've gone too far. Da has nae todger and ye know it. Mum keeps it tucked nicely in her sewing box wi' her escape-the-marriage money.

Shannon must be drunk. That's literally the only explanation I have for this. Todger? Come on.

Or Declan is punking me. Except he's not the type. That wouldn't be an efficient use of his time.

A red wall of pure rage fills me as I pull up the contact info from the text stream and call her. I hate this phone, something Mom got on a mystery shop. The font is huge, and the screen only shows last name, first initial.

The ring stops as the call is picked up, and I shout before she can say a word, "Are you drunk? What are you babbling about? Mom *actually* broke her femur and you're going on and on and–"

"Who the hell is this? C'mon, Darren. Ye can do better. Ye

got an American girl tucked in that hovel of a bedroom of yers and ye're using her to prank me? I'll tell ye what, pet, dinna look under his bed. The socks are balled up fer a reason. They died of sheer exhaustion."

"SHANNON?"

A pause.

"Ma name is Hamish McCormick. Not Shannon. Are ye with ma brother Darren?"

"This is Amy. How the hell are you on the phone with me, Hamish? How did you get Shannon's phone?"

"Hello, Amy. What're ye nattering on about? *Ye* called *me.*"

Ding!

I look at the screen. Text from Carol.

I knew it would happen eventually, but I thought it would be Dad who died during kinky stuff. Meet you at the hospital as soon as I can. BTW that's not Shannon's number.

"Hamish?" I squeak, cursing this stupid phone. How did I call *him?*

"Aye. And who're ye again? Amy? Darren has a new American girlfriend named Amy?"

"I have no idea who Darren is. This is Amy Jacoby. Shannon's sister. Declan's sister-in-law." It seems silly to explain myself to him. We were paired in my sister's wedding, walked down the aisle together as bridesmaid and groomsman. Before the wedding, Hamish booty-called me at three a.m. to talk about "how to use my hands on you."

So if I'm overexplaining myself, it's a purely defensive posture intended to distract him from the fact that *I'm* the idiot who accidentally called *him*.

"Aye. I know who ye are. Caller ID, ye know?"

"Then why did you pretend you didn't know who I was?"

"Because it was more fun that way."

"That's rude."

"In fact, I was just thinking about ye, Amy."

"Really? It's not three a.m., Hamish. Your timing's off."

Silence, then a burst of deep laughter that makes me hotter than an hour on the stair machine.

"So ye do remember."

"And why would you be thinking about *me* right now, Hamish?"

I slide behind the wheel and shove the key in the ignition, but stop myself from turning it. Driving while talking to an egotistical jerk who I've just accidentally told a very private detail about our family is only going to get me into an accident. I don't need to add yet another way that Hamish McCormick infuriates me.

His long pause is driving me nuts.

And then he says, "Oh, nae reason. And now I see it's fate."

"Fate?"

"Ye texted me about yer poor Da's willie. It's fate that it was me, and nae some stranger that would embarrass him even more."

"Embarrass *him*?"

"Nae man wants his daughter running around talking about his todger."

"I didn't do this by choice!"

"And I'm sorry about Marie. Broke her leg?" I feel his shudder through the phone. "That's the kiss of death fer footie players like me."

"Then don't have kinky sex and you'll be just fine."

"I'd rather give up ma leg than give up the kinky good stuff."

The leer in his voice isn't as sickening as it should be. In fact, it's...

Making me blush.

Hamish McCormick represents everything I cannot stand in a man. He's full of himself. Cocky. He approaches life with a blithe attitude that takes nothing seriously except pleasure.

What kind of life is *that?*

"I must say, Amy, that I'm surprised ye still have ma number in yer contacts. That says something, nae?"

Through gritted teeth, I answer, "All it says is that we were in Shannon and Declan's wedding together and I added it for emergencies."

"Sure," he says, drawing the word out. "But the wedding was years ago, and ye kept it?" A suggestive tone in his voice, flirty and light, makes my skin tingle. I don't want to like him. I truly don't.

But he has a point. Why didn't I delete him?

"Amy?"

"What?"

"Yer beamin."

"Beaming?"

"Ach, what's the word ye use? Blushing?"

"How would you know?"

"I can feel yer heat through the phone."

"Shut up!"

His laugh makes heat rise from every pore of my skin. Maybe he did feel it.

"Ye clearly miscalled me. Who're ye trying to reach?"

I put the phone on speaker, searching contacts.

Aha! I've mistyped Shannon McCormick as Hannon, the missing S putting her next to Hamish McCormick. I never should have accepted a free phone from one of my mother's mystery shops. A simple font problem and *bam!*–I'm on the phone with a talking testosterone syringe.

I quickly correct my error. Like all humans, I make mistakes.

Unlike most humans, *I* make them once, learn from them, and never, *ever* make the same mistake twice.

"I had Shannon in my contacts without the S. You're next to her, alphabetically," I explain.

"Ach. Good. Because when I thought it was ma younger

brother texting about Da's todger, I figured he went on a bender."

"I noticed."

"But if it's *ye* talking about a boaby, that's an entirely different matter." Voice dropping low and rich at the end, Hamish's innuendo ignites parts of me that have been in hiding for years.

Some of them, *forever*.

I have two options here: stammer or attack. I go for the latter.

"You are nothing but an uncontrolled impulse on two legs," I snap back. "Do you think about anything other than sex and soccer?"

There's a brief pause.

"It's *football*."

"No one is that shallow."

A throaty laugh, rumbling with the lilting tones of his Scottish accent, makes it that much harder to resist him. "If ye mean do I think o' naught but sex and football, I am justly accused."

"You are ridiculously infuriating."

"So much passion in ye fer me, Amy. I like that. I like it verra much."

I can practically hear him wink.

"There's more to life than sex and football!"

"Is there? I hadna noticed. Right now, ye've an abundance of both."

"WHAT?"

"Yer parents' sex life, and me, the footie player."

"You? There's no abundance of you in my life!"

"We could change that."

"Oh, no. No, no, no. I'm not falling for your lines, mister. I know what you are."

"What am I?"

"Dangerous." The word's out of my mouth before I can stop it.

Hamish's laughter fills my ear as I end the call.

Heart slamming in my chest, I press the phone against my breast.

It rings. I answer.

"I will never, ever, EVER sleep with you, so don't even try your flirty bullshit on me," I snap into the phone.

"Uh, sweetie? It's me," my dad says meekly.

Oh, hell.

"I—sorry, Dad! I thought you were Hamish."

"Hamish McCormick?"

"Do we know any other Hamishes?"

"No. But..."

"I don't want to talk about it. How's Mom?"

"She has a cast, a lot of pain pills, and she's muttering something about using cornstarch instead of flour when you make the gravy."

I inhale sharply. "That's blasphemy. Are you sure she didn't have a brain injury when she fell? Mom never uses cornstarch!"

"I know." He lowers his voice. "I think the accident has altered her somehow."

"Jason!" I hear through the phone. "Who's that?"

"It's Amy," he answers. A shuffling sound makes it clear I'm being handed off.

"Hi, honey," Mom says, voice dreamy and a little slurred. "Your dad and I made a boo boo."

"Right."

"Can you take care of Chuffy? He needs to pee."

"Of course."

"Your dad hurt my chuff when we were playing trapeze, like in *The Greatest Showman*. You know the really bendy woman in that movie? Turns out I'm not like her."

"Mom. MOM! I have to go. Love you!"

Pressing End Call never felt so good.

Bzzz

On my way in two minutes! It's Carol. She started a new group text, this time with Shannon's actual number.

This sounds bad. Let me guess: sex swing? Shannon texts.

How did you know? I reply. *Dad asked me to remove it before anyone sees it.*

Carol made a bet with me six years ago that one of them would die via sex swing, she types back.

Who bet on death? I ask, sidetracked.

Carol sends a thumbs-up emoji. *You owe me $100, Shannon,* she adds.

Nope! They're alive. We said death, not dismemberment or broken limbs.

Cheapskate. Amy, I'll clean up the house if you go to the hospital with Shannon and handle the Mom interface.

I pause.

And pause.

And pause for so long, Carol finally texts: *Hello?*

Still trying to decide which is worse, I finally answer: *Sure.*

The screen erupts with GIFs I don't want to even try to describe, but most of them involve sex swings.

Leave it to my sisters to find *those*.

And every single one of them makes me think of Hamish.

Damn it.

Hamish

"Hamish!" the old man bellows at me not five minutes after I'm off the call with Amy, a big voice coming from a wee phone. He's jocular and genial when he wants something from me.

Not money. Ach naw.

Me.

My uncle, billionaire James McCormick, wants *me*. I'm a commodity to him, like a bottle of fine whisky, or an Aston Martin.

It doesna bother me. Family is weird.

American family is even weirder.

"Hello, James. How they hanging?"

"Fine, fine," he says in that low tone of his. "And you?"

"Canna complain."

"Heard you're stuck in New York. Your agent called to let me know."

I groan inside. Jody. Jody's responsible for this. James

didn't reach out to my agent. It was the opposite. The convenient timing was a wee too coincidental to be a coincidence.

Jody is dead meat.

"I am. Trying to get away from the holiday."

"Thanksgiving? You have no plans?"

Alarm bells go off in my head. "Well, I wouldna say that," I hedge. "In fact–"

"Because I have a job for you. Three days in Boston on a photo and film shoot. Pays well."

He names an amount that makes James suddenly far, far more interesting.

American weirdness often has large dollar signs attached to it, I've noticed. At least in my family.

"Aye. Ma agent told me. Thank ye. What's the job?"

"Have you ever seen that series of commercials with the sophisticated man who has seen everything, done everything, and who promotes a brand of alcohol?"

"Aye."

"This is similar to that, but better."

"And ye want me to star in it?"

"Hah! Good one, Hamish. Hell, no. *I'm* the star. You're the younger man who learns from the pearls of wisdom that I dispense to you, as we dine at various Anterdec properties."

In other words: I'm his wingman, soon to be immortalized in a media campaign for all the world to see.

Eye candy, indeed.

But that dollar amount could solve a lot of problems back home for Mum and Da. Unlike the American McCormicks, the Scottish McCormicks aren't rich. My Da is seven years older than James, in his seventies, and still working. I send money home, but Da's a stubborn one. He and James are half brothers, but you wouldn't know it.

James only started really paying attention to us when I rose up the ranks in football.

My ego isn't so big that it can't handle a few scratches

here and there for the right price, as long as the pin doesn't actually pop it.

"Ye've spoken with ma agent, Jody Previte."

"My people have. Contract's ready to be signed if you agree."

"And when is the shoot?"

"We can do it this weekend. You're in the States already, and he told me you're stuck. Can't find a flight." His voice changes a bit. "I don't understand, though. Your private jet is grounded?"

What private jet? I think to myself, but I pause before I just blurt that out.

"Something like that."

"Your engine woes are my gain. You'll stay at my home in Back Bay, of course. We'll have some cocktail parties."

Which means I'm bait.

He'll use me like a big, fat wriggler on a hook.

"This comes out o' the blue, James. I thank ye, of course, but why so suddenly? What's happened wi' Anterdec to make ye want this?"

I suspect I know the answer. It's been in the news, for goodness' sake. His son Andrew, my cousin, resigned from the family company. No longer CEO, he's rebranding a chain of gyms. It's not because of the news that I know this, though.

I know because Andrew has hired me to be the spokesperson for *his* regional chain, as he works to take it national.

Jody handles all this. I assume there's no conflict of interest if it's all run through him.

I also suspect James is beating his son to the punch. Competition runs through the blood the McCormick family like fine, aged Scottish whisky.

"It's time," James says, cagey and gruff. "Time to take what I've built and acknowledge who built it."

"Ye."

"Me. Who better to be the face of Anterdec than a man who really *does* have it all?"

"Aye," I murmur. Da told me a long time ago that James was full of himself. Although *himself* wasn't the word he used.

Da is definitely onto something.

"You'll do it." The words aren't in the form of a question.

"Do..?"

"The ad campaign. We can be finished by next Monday. I have the crew ready."

"On a busy holiday weekend?"

"When you're important enough, people rearrange their schedules for you."

"Canna argue with that."

"Then it's settled?"

"Aye."

"Car or helicopter?"

"Excuse me?"

"Which do you prefer? Anterdec will send whichever."

"Which one is driven by a hot woman?"

He laughs. "I like how you think, Hamish. We're so similar."

"I'll drink to that when I see ye next, James."

Because I'll need to get knackered to get that idea out of my head.

"One of my girls will call to make arrangements. See you tomorrow."

He ends the call.

A text buzzes. It's Jody.

You accepted? he asks.

Aye. For that daily rate, I'll play the fool.

Exactly.

What do ye mean, exactly?

My phone rings.

"I mean that's exactly what the job is. Didn't you see the scripts?"

"What? Nae."

He groans. "Hamish! Don't you have a single shred of curiosity about these jobs?"

"Nae. I show up, I do what I'm told, look at the camera, and I make more money in a day than ma da makes in a month."

"You will be playing the fool. Literally. The whole point of the commercials is to have James be the smartest, most sophisticated man alive, and you're a dunce."

"Fine."

"Fine?"

"Aye. Why would that bother me?"

"Oh. Good." Relief fills his voice. "Because if you'll accept this job, I have some other offers that–"

"Dinna push yer luck, Jody."

"Okay. Bye."

And with that, I'm hired to be bait for James McCormick's hook.

Well-paid bait.

My phone buzzes. It's James.

I'm sending a car. The shoot starts Friday. You'll be done Monday. If you don't have plans for Thanksgiving, my son's crazy in-laws are hosting a large family gathering that requires a brief cameo from me. We could do some common man shots there. The house is a bit dilapidated and authentic.

His son's in-laws must mean Marie and Jason Jacoby. Jason's a fine man–the truly crazy one is Marie. The woman named her wee doggo *Chuffy*, for goodness' sake.

I wonder how poor Jason's willie is doing after that whole texting mess I was in with Amy.

James seems to have no idea about Marie's mishap, and I play along. But if the Jacoby family is hosting Thanksgiving, it means Amy will be there. Imagining her face when I appear on their threshold is delicious.

Something close to joy courses through me, the first shot of adrenaline I've had all day.

That's more like it.

Aye, I reply to James. *I'd be happy to come.*

Aye, indeed. Because if nothing else, when it comes to Amy Jacoby, having the upper hand is crucial.

Otherwise? I'm not the dangerous one.

She is.

Amy

Dad doesn't put his foot down very often, but when he does, he's all in, suddenly alpha, and nothing is going to change his mind.

Not even Mom at her worst.

We're back at the house, Mom's fracture bad, but not as catastrophic as originally feared. It's late Tuesday night, and she's trying to assert control, insisting that all of her plans for the holiday, made during a time when she didn't have a freaking *broken leg,* remain intact.

"But, Jason! This isn't fair! You know how much I love cooking big family dinners." She pouts and makes eye contact with Shannon, Carol, and me, her looks pointed and deliberate, as if she's summoning witching power and gathering her coven.

Without makeup, and in pain, Mom looks so worn, so depleted. Her dyed blonde hair hangs limp, freshly-threaded eyebrows arched nicely, the skin of her eyelids puffy. For someone who smiles all the time, her mouth sure is turned down, and worry radiates from her eyes.

"No, Marie, you're not cooking Thanksgiving dinner. The girls will do it, or we can just go to a nice restaurant instead. Why not let me book a table at the Wayside Inn? We've always wanted to try their Thanksgiving feast."

Mom inhales so sharply, she sounds like a penny whistle.

"What? Go out to a *restaurant* on Thanksgiving? I'd sooner dumpster dive for dye-free organic tampons behind the natural food store!"

Carol leans over and whispers, "When she uses analogies *that* specific, they scare me. I'm never using tampons from their bathroom cabinet again."

"No one's saying we have to go out, Mom," Shannon says in a soothing voice, half her face twitching from Carol's comment. "Why not have it catered?"

Dad lights up and gives Shannon a grateful look. "I love that idea!"

"Catered dinner for all those people with two days to go before Thanksgiving? We'll never find someone, and besides, that would break the bank," Mom scoffs.

"My treat!" Shannon calls out quickly. "Let me do this."

"No!" Mom insists, her voice cracking. She winces and strokes her thick cast. "I can't believe I broke my leg two days before Thanksgiving! I mean, the orgasm was absolutely worth it, Jason," she says to Dad, who turns redder than his hair. "But–"

"A catered affair would really impress your guests, Mom," I soothe her. "And with Shannon and Declan footing the bill, you could invite more people. Imagine how impressed Agnes and Corrine would be."

"Agnes and Corrine can't chew anymore. They basically drink their calories," Mom notes.

"Top-shelf liquor!" Carol interjects, on the same page with me. "Ice sculptures! Live turkeys! You name it, Mom, Shannon and Declan will do it!"

Shannon glares at us, but it's just a sibling reflex. Her husband is a money tree in human form.

No one in the world is luckier than my sister, who met a billionaire while mystery shopping in one of the bagel shops owned by Anterdec, the company her husband's father, James McCormick, built. While evaluating the cleanliness of the men's room, she was hiding in a stall to avoid being caught, but Declan came in, she dropped her cellphone in the toilet, and the rest is history.

History, a swallowed engagement ring, a Vegas escape from their own wedding when Mom went all Momzilla, a baby born in a broken elevator, and –

Hmm. Maybe she's not so lucky after all.

But all of that aside, Declan worships Shannon, and now we're all related to the family that created a Fortune 500 company, a Boston institution in and of itself.

"Catering? It's so impersonal! Thanksgiving is about having fun cooking with my girls, bonding and connecting, giggling and joking for hours as we bask in the glow of a beautiful day for extended family and friends," Mom gushes.

Carol, Shannon, and I all stop short.

"Since when?" we ask in unison.

Pretty sure Dad's baritone voice was in there, too.

Mom bursts into tears, her keening voice so quick, so shocking, I feel like someone shot me through the heart. Having been primed by parents like mine to feel so connected to family, it takes me a minute to find composure.

But I do.

People who are successful in the corporate world–and that's my goal–have to detach from emotion and focus on logic.

"Maybe if we have enough liquor, we can pretend for Mom's sake that cooking together is some bonding moment," Shannon suggests, earning a sincere nod from Carol, who is also taking this to heart.

"But Thanksgiving is in two days! The farm delivered the fresh turkeys today! I have to be able to shop for all the last-minute stuff!"

Mom's protests fall on deaf ears.

"Just have everything delivered, Mom. All the grocery stores do it now," Shannon shoots back.

"They can't pick out the perfect yams! Those shoppers don't know which crevices matter!"

Carol's lips form a pale line as she holds herself back from making a joke about crevices.

My eldest sister is so immature when it comes to sex.

Probably because she desperately needs some.

Mom continues. "I just started a six-week yoga series on Finding Your No! and we're doing a Woo Wednesday special *tomorrow*."

Dare I ask?

"Woo Wednesday?" I venture, quietly spelunking to find *my* no.

The no aimed at whatever scheme my mother is about to beg us to help with.

"The day before Thanksgiving. Lots of energy healers, yoga studios, and massage therapists are offering deep discounts to compete with Black Friday."

"Look, we can't handle the yoga," Carol starts, "but the three of us have Thanksgiving covered. Shannon and Declan will pay for everything. Dad will smoke one of the turkeys."

"Of course!" he bellows.

"Yes!" Shannon shouts.

"And Shannon and Declan can buy all the liquor, beer, and wine, too. Have it delivered," Carol adds.

"Yep!" Shannon says, obviously relieved to have Dad and Mom willing to accept some of the money she now has. Mom accepts it more regularly, but Dad is too proud.

We're enthusiastically trying to make Mom feel better, but the sinking feeling in my stomach isn't fading. She's going to insist we have a 'normal' Thanksgiving, which is already four-teen hours of back-breaking labor.

But she's not one of the laborers this year, so her share falls on us.

"I don't know," Mom says, still skeptical. Her hair is a bedhead mess, probably from a mixture of sex earlier today, and all the hospital time. Without makeup, she looks so old. Beaten down and tired.

Marie Jacoby never looks like this. It's disconcerting. Plus, she's high on pain meds, and her whole demeanor is different.

Sure, her personality is there. Stubbornness is the last characteristic to fade, I imagine.

And Mom has all the stubborn-ness genes.

Which she passed on to her girls.

"There's no way I am cancelling my yoga class. So many of those women need it. The stress of the holiday is immense. And then there are the women who don't get to see their kids for Thanksgiving, and really need the connection," Mom says in a sad whisper. Is she tearing up?

Carol, Shannon and I look at each other in alarm.

Fix this, Carol mouths to me and Shannon.

I shrug.

How? I mouth back.

Shannon picks up her phone and starts texting. "I know a yoga teacher who can help you, Mom."

"Who?"

"Terry."

"Terry who?"

"You know, Declan's older brother. Terry."

"*Terry McCormick* teaches *yoga?*" Carol's voice tells me more than I want to know about how she feels toward our brother-in-law's brother. With that tone of voice and her features, she looks and sounds exactly like Mom when she's leering.

Shannon squints at her screen as she pokes. "Yep," she explains. "He said he went to so many classes, he decided it would be fun to gain more mastery. Got some kind of certification."

"Spoken like someone who has no kids, no job, and a trust fund," Carol comments.

Shannon shoots her a hurt look. "Don't sound so judgy."

"I'm not judging! I'm *admiring!*"

"You know," Dad says softly, puppy-dog eyes full of regret and sadness for Mom, "I'm the one who did this. I should shoulder the burden."

We all go quiet.

Not because Dad's being particularly poignant.

Because DEAR GOD, NO, WE DO NOT WANT TO HEAR MORE ABOUT EXACTLY HOW MOM BROKE HER LEG.

"You can't do it all, Jason! It's too much." Mom winces as she twists to talk to him.

His chin goes up in defiance. "I can. If I do it my way, I can."

"What do you mean, *your* way? We do it *our* way every year."

"No, Marie. We don't."

Everyone in the room who is their progeny goes still.

Is... is... is Dad standing up to Mom?

"We–what are you talking about, Jason?" She picks up a prescription bottle from the end table next to her and squints at the label. "These drugs must be *goooooood*, because I could swear you just said we don't do Thanksgiving our way."

"We don't. No drugs needed. We do the holiday your way, and always have."

Thud.

That's the sound of my father finding his balls.

It's louder than I'd expect.

"Jason," Mom groans. "Why are you doing this to me?"

"I'm not. I'm doing this *for* you. Relax, Marie. Let me be in charge, for once. You don't have to carry the burden all the time."

"But who *am* I if I'm not making the holiday dinner? And no one does it better than me."

"How can you possibly know that? You've never let anyone but you run the show."

Thud.

That's the sound of my mother's eyeballs bugging out of her head and hitting the floor.

"Excuse me? No one else offers!" That's not even remotely true, but Dad is an expert at dodging red herrings.

"I'm offering now, Marie. Let me handle this. Let go and trust me."

"Why would I trust you after you did this to me?" She gestures at her leg. "If you'd listened to me, none of this would have happened. I told you the coconut oil-based lube was too slippery for putting Mr. Wet Hug inside my–"

"MOM!" we all shout, unified by our desperate desire to stop seeing them having kinky sex in our mind's eye.

Nothing makes squabbling siblings come together for a cause like *that* does.

Plus, really? Did we have to learn Mom's nickname for Dad's, um...

"You don't trust me?" Dad's voice cracks, and so does my world.

Mom and Dad don't fight. They don't argue. Sure, once in a while, they snip at each other. Or Mom natters on and pokes him in a sore spot and they get tense. But fight? Like this?

No.

"Of course I trust you, Jason! But this is different."

"How?"

"There are thousands of tiny details that only live in my head. What am I supposed to do if I'm not in charge? Sit around and watch football all day while everyone waits on me hand and foot?"

"YES!" we all shout at her.

"I don't even like football!" she wails. "I only watch it because Tom Brady's butt is so adorable in those tight pants."

"Mom," Carol says, bending down on one knee, taking Mom's hand in hers and using her other hand to pat the giant leg cast. "You have to accept this."

"No, I don't."

"You can't ignore reality," Carol replies.

Shannon and I snort, then pretend to cough.

"Look, we can do this the easy way, or the hard way," Carol says.

"What's the easy way?" Mom asks with an eye roll.

"Let us do Thanksgiving *our* way," Carol replies.

"What's the hard way?"

"We carry you into the basement and throw protein bars and bottled water down the stairs once a day until you stop screaming."

"I have very strong lungs. I'd outlast you."

"We can buy really, really good earplugs with all of Shannon's money."

Mom's eyes go flat and cold, but I see something else there: fear. Obviously, she's not afraid Carol will do what she's joking about doing. She's afraid to give up control of Thanksgiving.

Why?

"Marie. It's one year. You can climb right back in the saddle next year," Dad ventures.

"Oh, ho, ho, ho–no, Jason! We have that saddle you bought last year, but after what happened with the swing, I'm done with anything in which I have to defy gravity to have an orgasm!"

"That was a euphemism, honey."

"Oh."

"You can cook Thanksgiving next year. And the year after that. And all the years until you die, Mom," Shannon says, kneeling down like Carol. They look like ladies at court, appeasing their queen.

I'm the odd woman out, still standing.

And I intend to keep it that way.

"Think of it this way, Mom," I say, mind churning to find the bit of persuasion that will convince her. In business, people who can close a shaky deal are held in high regard. It takes a certain kind of emotional intelligence to scan an undecided person's mental state, home in on the source of their indecision, then determine the best approach to alleviate their concerns and convince them to take action that meets your needs, yet also meets theirs.

"Just think, if we get it right, you'll never have to do holiday dinners again!"

Mom turns red with fury.

"WHAT?"

Oops.

I need to pivot. *Fast.*

"I mean, let us do it our way this one time. I'll bet it'll prove to everyone that *your* way is best."

Carol stands and turns to me, mouthing *Perfect*.

Mom's eyes light up. "Do you really mean it?"

"Yes," I say, because I do. I do mean it. No matter what, Mom will think her way is the only way to do Thanksgiving. Getting her to sit it out this year is the goal here.

Not trying to make her see there's a better way.

"But there's one requirement," Shannon adds. "You cannot interfere. We're doing it our way, and you can only watch."

"But I – "

"No," Shannon cuts in firmly. "You cannot cook a single thing."

"With an office chair on wheels I can – "

"NO!"

Eyes narrowing, Mom looks at each of us in turn, slowly and deliberately.

"I'll accept some of your terms, but with one requirement: you have to let me influence behind the scenes."

"What does that mean?" I ask.

"Have some input," she says, her eyes going unfocused, the drugs really kicking in.

Carol, Shannon, Dad and I exchange looks. A shrug from Dad makes us all relent.

"Okay," Shannon says in a slow, skeptical tone. "But no cooking."

"Fine. You have a deal." She looks at Shannon. "You need to get Terry on the line. I have a lot of explaining to do about my yoga class."

Dad runs a shaking hand through his thinning hair, the same shade of auburn as mine, though he has enough grey sprinkled in there to give it a lighter look.

"Good girl," he whispers to me as Shannon makes the call and hands her phone to Mom, who begins speaking into it animatedly.

"I don't know about that. She's incapable of not butting in."

"I know."

"Shannon, Carol, you, and I just signed ourselves up for a job we weren't expecting, and we'll be fighting Mom every step of the way. How many are coming for dinner, anyway?"

"I don't know, honey. And I need a beer before we start the planning."

"I'll get my laptop, bullet journal, and colored pens. Oooh, and color-coded post-its, and a kanban board!" I announce, because the only way to manage unexpected chaos is by having the right tools.

And colors.

Dad groans.

Suddenly, this is looking kind of interesting–maybe even fun. If I organize it well enough, I really *can* do a better job than Mom. I can impose order on chaos. I mean, when you think about it, what is a large family event if not a management challenge?

If I were at work doing my co-op, how would I take a disorganized mess and smooth it out?

With an organized plan. A detailed to-do list. Proper resource allocation.

I am going to project-manage this mess into a crowning achievement.

By the time this holiday is over, Mom will be forced to admit that we've done it better.

I have my work cut out for me.

3

Hamish

The old man's townhouse in Back Bay is like a parody of an English manor house's library–the whole place. It's like he took an old Edinburgh pub, combined it with Downton Abbey, and added a bit of Madame Tussaud's wax museum for good effect.

Aged leather, antique Persian rugs, dark-stained oak, and a bleakness that comes from having a soul composed of bits and pieces of humanity patched together with money.

I know the stories from Da about how my uncle James grew up poor on the streets of South Boston, scraping together enough to buy some rat-infested warehouses he turned into apartments later. Building by building, he leveraged his money into more and more.

Then he fell in love with an heiress, married her, had three sons, and Anterdec–now a Fortune 500 company–was born.

Not many people can go from rags to riches with an intact

psyche, and James is no exception. There's an aloofness to him, with a jaw-grinding arrogance as he throws his weight around, assuming the world will do his bidding.

I'm his wingman. An ornament. A person he collects because he thinks being surrounded by success validates his own. You don't need to be stinking rich to do this. I know some poor people back in Glasgow who do it, as if someone else's success is somehow contagious. Rub a bit of it on you through direct contact and the rest of the world will think more of you.

Never understood it. I don't measure my worth in terms of who I'm around. The measure of me, as a person, is what I *do*.

"Going somewhere?" James asks me as I stretch in his kitchen, a protein shake in my stomach, bottled water on the marble counter. It's late November in Boston, but a 10K run means I'll sweat, so I'm in trainers, shorts, and a long-sleeved compression t-shirt.

"Need to run. Have a strict workout schedule."

His eyes comb over me. "I see why. Peak athletes have to be disciplined."

"Aye."

"When I was coaching Andrew for the Olympics, he was a machine. A swimming machine. That boy could do whatever we pressed him to do. Then he threw it all away."

The dismissive tone gets to me.

"He tried his best," I say, keeping it light, finishing my calf stretch, now eager to go.

"Trying is for losers. No one gets the gold for trying, Hamish," James snorts. "I'm surprised to hear that *try* crap from you. Your coach tolerates that?"

"Ma manager is too busy keeping players out of the *Sun* scandal pages to worry about what I say, James. He's all about what we *do*."

"I like do-ers. Not try-ers. When will you be back?"

" 'bout forty-five minutes."

"Good. Declan and Andrew are coming by."

I brighten. *Whew*. James is a bit much on his own. Good to spread the joy about with others.

I wave as I leave, and his mouth twists in a weird smile that makes me wonder if being here is such a good idea after all.

The run will clear my head.

Urban running in America is not much different than at home, with people walking dogs, mums with pushchairs, and the fast-marching suits on their way to move money around on computer networks.

The older cities have more varied terrain. In Boston, some streets are still paved with cobblestones. My ankles aren't loving the uneven ground, so different from a football pitch, but the variation builds flexibility and strength.

You need to give all the tiny muscles a chance to prove their worth. And ache a little, so you know they're ready for high performance.

While I don't agree with James that there's something wrong with the word *try*, I get his point. You don't reach the top of your profession, especially sports, without going above and beyond. An intolerance for losing is a predictor of success.

It's why I'm running 10K right now, and finishing it up in forty minutes or so. It's why I do Pilates, yoga, strength training, and more. After all the players have been running around for ninety minutes, with the game on the line, I need to still have that extra burst of speed. My fans expect it.

Conditioning isn't just about making sure all the different parts of the body work together.

It's about reminding your body that every piece of it matters.

A flash of long, auburn hair on a woman I run past makes me do a double take.

No. Not Amy Jacoby.

On long runs, the mind wanders. It seeks something to latch onto and mull over for a bit, to pass the time. And there are far worse subjects I could think about than Amy Jacoby.

She's a fiery beauty, with an emphasis on the blaze.

Women like her avoid me.

Sounds crazy, I know, but it's true. I know her type, and they stay away. No, she's not afraid. And yes, she's attracted to me.

But someone like her has a wall, a near stone fortress, around her. All I'll get are polite greetings, small talk, and silent stares.

Because Amy Jacoby has decided that I'm a cocky, brainless, no-substance man who isn't worth her respect.

We first met at Shannon and Declan's apartment, when they were getting married and Shannon hosted a rehearsal dinner party. Marie dressed the groomsmen and the groom in more tartan than Burberry for that wedding. It looked like someone took the McCormick tartan, sent it to a Chinese factory to be imprinted on every product imaginable, and we bought it all.

Even the wee tissue packets they handed out for the crying women had tartan on them.

Pretty sure the whisky had tartan labels.

Marie has no filter. Meeting her was like peeling off a drunk church lady at the corner pub after the hot priest was reassigned to London and she's crying in her beer.

At a traffic light, I jog in place and check the running route. Five more minutes.

Another redhead.

She's across the street and gives me a look. We gingers are rare, so we tend to smile at each other, wave, or even chat.

A look comes over her that I know all too well: celebrity recognition.

"Hamish McCormick?" she calls from across the street. "*The* Hamish McCormick? From AFC Dunsdill?"

"Aye!" I shout back, pleased to be recognized in America. Back home, I can't walk a block on the Royal Mile without peeling fans away.

Here? Not so much.

The redhead opens her mouth and yells in an accent I can't place, but it's somewhat north of London, "You totally blew that goal last week! What were you thinking?"

"It bounced off the crossbar!" I shout back, but she gives me the finger.

Hmph. I even have haters in Boston. That's progress.

I wave and change my route as she screams insults, the last one something about not being able to find the goal even if I had both hands, a flashlight, Diogenes' lantern, and a phosphorus torch.

Always good to find a true fan.

The streets are thicker with people now, so I spend more time dodging than running. By the time I'm back at James's place, I'm dripping with sweat and nursing a hurt ego.

But not for long. My ego is self-regenerating.

You cannot have thin skin and play football. It's impossible. The guys who are too weak willed weed themselves out quickly. Learning to ignore the nasties and just play is one of the hardest parts of the job.

You try screwing up the thing you're good at in front of twenty thousand people who all start booing you, and see how good that feels.

That's why Amy's disgust with me doesn't get under my skin.

In fact, it piques my curiosity.

Why? Why does a woman who has no earthly reason to hate me, *hate* me?

Only one explanation.

Lust.

The front door opens before I even press the buzzer, James himself opening it.

"Declan and Andrew are here. Come in, come in."

The ends of my hair are wet. My socks are soaked. The run wasn't hard, but I did it fast, which always gets my blood boiling.

"I need a quick shower."

"No time," Andrew says, shaking my hand but not coming in for a hug. I don't blame him.

"Nae time?"

"If you're free," Declan says as I shake his hand in turn, "we're on our way to watch our brother make a fool of himself."

"Aye, I'm always up fer a good public spectacle."

And to escape from James for a bit, if possible.

James scoffs. "What's Terry up to now? Did he join the Hari Krishnas?"

"He's teaching Marie's yoga classes for her for a few weeks."

"Same thing," James grouses.

"How?" I ask.

Andrew frowns, dark brows going thick over his eyes. "By... teaching yoga."

"Na. I mean why's he teaching her class?"

"She broke her leg."

James makes a pained face, the first bit of empathy I've seen him express for anyone. "Ouch. How?"

Declan's expression can only be described as chagrined disgust. "Don't ask, Dad."

"Why not?"

"Do you *really* want to know, Dad?"

"No," James says flatly, picking up on the cue.

"Poor Amy," Andrew says as Declan looks about as comfy as a sick coo. "She was the one who took the call from Jason."

"Amy?" I ask. "I was just talking wi' her."

"You were?" All three men ask the question in the exact same tone.

"She called me the other day."

"She did?" Andrew's question comes with a bit of a leer. "Amanda says she's had her eye on you for a while."

Declan elbows him and tries to cut a gleeful Andrew in half with a glare.

"What? Wouldn't it be funny if they ended up together? What did Marie say years ago, at your rehearsal dinner, Dec? Hamy and Amy?" Andrew adds with a sharp tone that tells me he's telling the truth.

Which makes my blood rush a bit.

"Don't call me that," I snap. "Unless ye want to be called Andy and Mandy."

I get a nonverbal handwave that makes it clear we understand each other.

"We're going to be late, *Andy*," Declan says to his brother, who accepts a folder of papers from James. I suspect that's the real reason they're here–business, of course.

Inviting me to a yoga class run by Terry is secondary. These McCormicks are all business, all the time. I can't decide whether I like it or not.

Have to admire it, though. Ruthless and determined, they're competitive and successful.

Like me.

"I'll come. Sounds like fun, and I could use the workout."

"You just ran six miles!" James says in an appreciative tone, one he uses less to flatter me and more as a weapon, giving Andrew a look. "Remember when *you* used to work out this hard? When you were in the Olympic trials? Speaking of that, how're the twins' swimming lessons coming along? Any natural talent in either of them?"

"Dad, they're two years old."

"You can tell by that age."

"We're not having this conversation." Andrew's words are cold and unyielding. If I talked to my Da like that, I'd get a backhand. Maybe a remote thrown at my head. Definitely a biscuit or two.

But my Da isn't James, either. My father will talk to you about who you are, who you know, how you interact with people, with the community. We were raised to think of family as people who drive you crazy, but you love them anyhow. And we all have each other's back. It's why all the money I make for doing something that comes naturally is so important. I send most of it home to raise up my old neighborhood, and plenty to help Mum and Da.

But all this talk is making my body twitch. I need movement.

"Let's go watch yer brother in all his warrior-pose glory," I say, walking to the front door as James snorts.

"He could have been CEO of Anterdec. Instead, he's teaching old ladies how to keep their calf muscles from spasming."

"The world needs men to do both," I reply, trying to lighten the mood, but James just gives me a dour look before turning away without another word.

"Oh, he's a fun one," I mutter to Declan as we walk down the stone steps. There's a black Tesla Model X parked at the curb. The doors unlock and we climb in, Andrew at the wheel.

As he pulls out into traffic, Andrew says casually, "Amy might be there."

"Aye?"

"So why'd she really call you? You two have something going on on the side?"

"Nae. It was an accident. She meant to call Shannon to tell her about how their Da almost broke his penis doing something kinky on a sex swing. It's how Marie broke her leg."

A long, slow groan comes out of Declan. "Shannon didn't tell me *how* Marie broke her leg. I figured it was bad, but not *sex swing* bad. Shannon just said that she and her sisters have to handle Thanksgiving dinner now."

"The turkey day that got me stuck here," I sigh.

"How'd you get stuck?" Andrew asks.

"Nae flights home. Stupid holiday made it impossible."

"Not a single seat available?" Declan asks, but before I can answer, Andrew interrupts.

"What about private jet?"

"Are ye joking?" He's driving, so I can't look him in the eye, but I know he's not joking, and he knows the question is one that changes the balance of power.

"Got it."

"How goes the gym business?" I ask, knowing this is a topic he'll enjoy. "Ma agent is lining up the details for the endorsement campaign with yer gyms."

A grin transforms his face, the man so self-contained and serious. Declan's worse, though. Andrew has a true relationship with James, even if it's a bit prickly. Declan and his father, though, that's a frosty one.

And it makes Declan cool and hard to read.

"It's good. We're trying to convince Old Jorg to play a bit role in the marketing rollout," Andrew explains.

"If yer aiming fer a younger crowd, what's the point?"

"Old Jorg conveys an authenticity. Vince says people don't want bunny gyms."

"Bunny gyms?"

"You know. Fluff and buff places. My chain is authentic. Real."

"Really stinky," Declan mutters.

Andrew frowns and gives me a look in the rearview mirror. "You changed the topic. We're not finished talking about you and Amy."

"What about me and Amy?"

"Amanda told me you hit on her during Declan's wedding."

I can't help but laugh. "I hit on everyone, Andrew. Nae surprise there. She's a pretty one, so..."

"But nothing came of it?"

"She shot me down."

"And you didn't try again?"

"Aye. I did. But she's a wily one."

"*Amy?* Amy isn't wily. She's just... Amy. Shannon's kid sister," Declan points out.

"That 'kid' is twenty-nine and about to get her MBA, Dec," Andrew reminds him.

"Sure. She's more business-minded than Carol or even Shannon," Dec concedes. "But *wily?* What do you mean, Hamish?"

"I may no' know much about business, but I do know a lot about women, if ye get ma drift," I say with a wink. "And Amy is the type of woman ye dinna woo easily. She takes time."

"You're wooing her?"

"I woo everyone. But na. I'll tease her, joke wi' her, but I'm not trying to shag her. No' with any... determination."

"Why not?" Andrew's simple question is genuine. Curious.

There's a physical sensation that hits me when I need to move my body. It's subtle, then strong. Out of the blue, I have to move. *Have* to.

It's happening now.

My muscles tighten, the squeeze impossible to bear. For some reason, answering Andrew's question is making my body react like this, and I'm trapped in a car.

Trapped.

"I dinna want to muddy the family waters," I reply, the words wrong but good enough. "Na one needs bad blood there. Nae 'Hamy and Amy.'"

"You mean if it didn't work out?" Declan's voice is casual, but he's a sharp one.

"I'm still stuck on Amy being wily," Andrew muses.

There's a lump in my throat I don't like, and my heart starts pumping like mad. It's not left over from the run. Teammates don't talk like this. No one asks me how I feel about a hen.

They ask how it felt to be *in* her, not how it feels to *fall* for her.

"Amy's the kind of woman ye have to win over, and by the time ye exhaust yerself with the chase, she has na respect for ye. No winning with that one. Ye know the type, aye?"

They nod.

"Shannon and Amanda aren't like her."

The air goes cold with my comment. Shite.

"What does that mean?" Declan asks. I'm in the back seat, sitting behind Andrew, and his eyes catch mine in the rearview mirror.

"It means ye knew ye wanted them from the first moment ye met, aye?"

Both let out grunts.

I'll take that as a yes.

"And they felt the same. Then ye did the mating dance. But the moment ye met them, ye knew. Just... knew. And here ye are, marrit wi' bairns."

"You're describing love at first sight," Declan points out.

"Aye."

"I didn't love Amanda the first time I met her," Andrew says slowly. "It was at the same meeting where Dec and Shannon realized they were Hot Guy and Toilet Girl."

Declan laughs. "Haven't heard those terms in a while."

"There was a spark, though? Something that caught yer eye?" I persist. Have to. Something in me won't let go.

"Sure."

"Did ye ever feel like ye had to win her over?"

"No."

"See?"

"See what?"

"That's the difference. Amy's got walls."

"Walls?"

"Big ones. Stone walls built into a mountain. Being wi' her is like scaling Edinburgh Castle wi' yer bare hands and feet. It's a lot of effort and in the end, yer bloody, bruised, and exhausted."

"Isn't love worth the effort?"

"Love! Who said anything about me and Amy and love?"

"You just did."

"She hates me. Thinks I'm naught but a walking sex stick."

Both men burst into raucous laughter.

"I dinna understand why that's a bad thing," I add.

Truly.

"Then this yoga class should be fun," Andrew says. He turns on some old seventies music and the car is filled with electric guitar, drums, and the sound of my heart beating.

Hard.

Amy

"Those tights are giving you camel toe, Amy."

Apparently, it's not enough that I'm being forced to attend a yoga class taught by my brother-in-law's black sheep brother. I also have to pass my mother's inspection of acceptable attire.

We're getting ready to head over to Mary Elizabeth's renovated chicken coop where Mom teaches yoga. For a woman who broke her leg twenty-four hours ago, who is defying doctor's orders, and who has more than twenty guests coming to the house tomorrow, her insistence on attending "Woo Wednesday" yoga is infuriating.

Because it obligates me, Carol, and Shannon to come and do damage control.

"Excuse me?"

"There is a lot going on in your nether regions." Mom waves at my midsection like Keith Lockhart conducting the Boston Pops holiday concert.

"No, there isn't!"

"She's telling the truth, Mom," Carol cracks. "There really isn't anything going on in Amy's nether regions. It's a barren desert."

"Hey!"

"Am I wrong?"

"Barren desert is a bit much."

"Frozen tundra more like it?"

"Shut up."

I take in Carol's outfit: a t-shirt from a local ice cream shop, a pair of baggy shorts, and tie-dye socks.

"You look like someone who's had the flu for three days, run out of clean clothes, and ate potato chips and chocolate syrup squirted straight in your mouth for dinner last night."

"Remove the flu part, and you're right," she snaps back at me, but her expression sours.

"Have you considered wearing yoga tights?"

"Why would I inflict that sight on the world?"

"Um, because it would cover the fur on your legs? You look like you haven't shaved since Tyler was born."

"The water at my house is shut off today! Leak on the main line into our subdivision. I was going to do a load of laundry and take a shower this morning." She winces, touching her hair, which is pulled back in a tight ponytail. She's wearing makeup.

More makeup than one would usually put on for a yoga class.

"Maybe I shouldn't go," she ponders.

"You look fine," I assure her, but I feel an evil smile on the inside. Carol's worry tells me a lot about how she feels about Terry.

This is fodder for teasing. Youngest sisters like me eat this up.

"Mom?" she calls out. "Does the yoga studio have a shower, by any chance?"

I know the answer to this one. "No," I inform her as her face falls. "Mary Elizabeth is renovating next year to add showers and a sauna, though."

"Fat lot of good that does me today."

"Why not do laundry and shower here?"

"Because the town kept saying water would be turned on and by the time I had to leave, it was too late."

"Girls! Let's get going," Mom calls out from her spot on the couch, leg poking straight out like a battering ram.

"We're trying!" Carol whines. "But Amy wants me to wear yoga pants!"

"Why on Earth would she insist on *that?*"

"HEY!" Carol bellows. "My ass isn't *that* bad!"

"Sorry!" Mom chirps. "I just meant it would delay us."

"Us?" Carol asks in a voice that tells me she doesn't know Mom's coming.

Yet again, our mother has selectively told people exactly what she wants them to know so that she is at maximum advantage to achieve her goals.

Regardless of what it does to us.

"You think I'm missing my own yoga class? I'm coming with you!"

"This was never part of the plan," I remind Mom, emboldened by Carol's presence. If there's a shred of a chance that we can dissuade her, it's worth trying.

More like rearranging the deck chairs on The Titanic, but whatever.

"Mom," Carol says in the calm tone of someone accustomed to talking to unstable people, small children experiencing tantrums, and customers who take being 'always right' to extremes, "you can't do yoga. You have a full leg cast."

"I'm not going to do the poses! I need to be there in case Terry has a problem."

"Terry is an intelligent, competent man who can handle teaching an hour-long yoga class in a converted chicken coop studio filled with a bunch of old women," Carol insists.

"My class is not just old women," Mom huffs. "We have a wide array of ages."

"Sure. Old, older, and Agnes," Carol replies.

"They all have fun, stay younger, and most important, they pay their fees. My classes are becoming so popular, I'm making almost double what I used to make. Do you have any idea how many people enjoy yoni yoga?"

Carol and I freeze.

"Mom," I ask, gritting my teeth, hating that I even have to ask. "Is Terry teaching your yoni yoga class?"

"And if yes, is he aware of this?" Carol adds.

Seconds tick by as we wait anxiously. If Terry's been roped into teaching a yoga class involving opening your vagina to elevate the portal to your sacred soul to a higher vibration, then he's in for a big surprise.

"No! Of course not. It's simple restorative yoga for Woo Wednesday. Yoni steaming is optional."

"I'm sure Terry will appreciate not having to steam his yoni."

"Carol!"

"Really, Mom? *That* bothered you? Of all the things we've just discussed, *that's* the one you object to?"

"We're going to be late," she grouses. "How am I going to fit in the car with this cast?"

"We can bungee cord you to the roof, like Dad does with the Christmas tree every year."

"Ha ha. Where's Shannon? I want my *nice* daughter to drive me. At least I managed to have *one*. I wouldn't put it past you two to tie me to Tyler's skateboard and drag me behind the car the whole way."

Carol gives me a look that says, *Is that an option?*

"Shannon and Amanda are meeting us at the yoga studio."

"Are Declan and Andrew coming?"

"Why would they?"

"I asked Shannon to get them to come."

"I'm sure they're way too busy."

"You would think they'd come to provide moral support for their own brother," Mom pouts. "If not to come see me in my hour of need."

"Your whole yoga career is nothing but a series of hours of need, especially when it comes to getting billionaires to attend your yoga classes, Mom," Carol shoots back.

"And the last thing Declan and Andrew are doing is *supporting* Terry," I add.

"What does that mean?" Mom fishes around in her lap, pulls out a prescription bottle, and dry swallows two pills.

Carol's jaw drops. "Mom, when have you ever known the McCormick brothers to support each other? If they come, it'll be to make fun of Terry."

"But then they'll at least be there! My class loves when they join in."

"'Join in,'" I say, using finger quotes. "More like when they're coerced."

"No one coerces them! It's a great workout. Declan and Andrew are fathers now. They need to stay in shape."

"Driving all the way to Mendon from Boston for an hour

workout a few times a year isn't going to help their physiques much, in the grand scheme of things," I note.

"The McCormick men do have good genes in that regard," Mom muses. "James is in his mid-sixties and still in fine shape. And then there's that Scottish cousin, Hamish."

Carol gives me a glance, then grins slowly, like she's savoring every second of my discomfort.

"Amy! You're blushing!" she says, purposely drawing Mom's attention to me.

"No, I'm not!"

"You are, dear," Mom notes. "I just mentioned Hamish, and it's obvious you have a thing for him."

"Do not!"

"See, Mom? Her face got redder." Carol pauses, then says, "Hamish."

My face is on fire.

"Oh, I see it!" Mom exclaims. "Your face is a mood ring!" She winks. "A Scottish mood ring."

I knock on her cast. "Where's Tyler's skateboard and a roll of duct tape?"

Mom pauses, then says, "The duct tape is in your father's night stand drawer."

Not even going to ask why.

Carol laughs. "We hit a nerve, Mom. Amy has a thing for Hamish."

"I cannot stand that useless bag of skin-covered air. There's no substance. He's all ego and legs," I shoot back.

"You *really* like him," Carol purrs.

"Does Tyler have two skateboards?" I grab the keys to Dad's minivan and storm off, fed up with their teasing. Carol can push Mom in her wheelchair and get her settled in the van.

I'm done.

Except... I'm not. Not done with Hamish McCormick. Now that they've brought him up, he's in my head. Again.

In my blood. Again.

In my–well, he's *everywhere*.

Why does someone I hate so much get under my skin like this?

The first time I ever saw him was at Shannon's wedding rehearsal dinner. Tall and handsome, he had those thick, soccer player legs that have muscles on muscles where the thigh meets the knee. And he was a redhead like me, with those dashing green McCormick eyes.

Shannon had told me he was famous in Europe, so I'd Googled him.

And needed a decontamination shower afterward.

Sex. The stories about him involved nothing but sex.

You'd think they'd be about soccer–*football*–but *noooooo*.

The guy wasn't just a human Petri dish, he was an entire infectious disease lab. With an underground deep-freeze containment center.

What kind of inner pain did this guy have, to be dipping his wick into every hole he could find in Europe?

Our first meeting wasn't exactly a warm welcome to the family.

And then there was that booty call. I guess it's totally predictable for an usher to hit on the bride's sister, the woman he's paired with for the ceremony, but at three a.m.?

What was Mr. Infectious Disease Lab doing earlier in the evening?

I am not going to think about that call right now. How his voice sounded. My shock at the phone ringing at that hour in the morning. My… okay, my *pleasure* at being desired by someone so desirable.

And I'm definitely not going to think about my regret at shooting him down, because that's some kind of short-circuit in my brain. Turning him down–profanity included–was the only smart thing to do.

Right?

Carol spends the next ten minutes turning Mom into a piece of human origami, somehow connecting the seat belt around her as she sits across the middle row of the van, cast on the seat.

"I'm going to get so carsick," she says in a worried tone.

"Perfect reason for a quiet ride. Let's listen to WICN and some smooth jazz."

I turn the radio on.

"I love WICN! It's what Jason and I listen to when we're making love."

I turn the radio off.

Carol and Mom get into an animated conversation about double coupons at Shaw's supermarket while I drive to the converted chicken coop that houses Mom's studio. A friend of hers renovated the place—a chicken coop nicer than our family home—and leases it to her for the handful of yoga classes Mom teaches.

She has her niche, for sure.

As I turn into the parking area, there are more people clutching canes than there are cars. One of those small buses from The Ride, our area's transportation system for the elderly and disabled, is just pulling out.

And then there's Agnes and Corrine.

I have no idea why my mother loves those weird, cranky ladies so much. They fight more than Carol and Mom, which is saying something. Agnes looks like a prune that's been run over a few times by a Zamboni, peeled off the ground, and dressed in an outfit from the back cover of an AARP magazine. Then painted with bright coral lipstick.

She's leaning on a walker.

"Agnes," Corrine protests as a woman about my age with long, dark hair in a ponytail grabs a second walker from her car trunk. "You're using my walker." She points to the one in the younger woman's hands. "That's yours!"

"Does it matter?" the young woman mutters, clearly tired of these two.

"Yes, Cassie, it sure does!" Corrine squawks. "Mine doesn't have nasty olive juice all over the handle."

"Don't you dare olive shame me, Corrine! I make a mean dirty martini and you're just jealous."

"Jealous? You've become a drunk, Agnes. A drunk with sticky bars on your walker. It's gross. If I wanted to have my hands covered with salty oil, I'd go to that O Spa in Boston and hire myself one of their stripper massage guys."

Carol's in the middle of unfolding Mom's wheelchair and comes to a dead halt.

"O Spa," she says, eyes softening with the recall of a porny memory. "That place is nirvana." She frowns at Corrine. "When have you ever been there?"

Corrine pretends to lock her lips with a key and toss it at Agnes's head. "I'll never tell, but let me say this: That Zeke guy with the British accent is a wild tiger."

"You're right about that, at least," Agnes chuckles.

"You are so gross, Grandma!" Cassie shakes her head.

I look at Mom.

Now I get it. I totally understand why she likes them so much. The old ladies are a preview of Mom in thirty or forty years.

Corrine and Agnes rush over to Mom–if shuffling their feet like a sloth racing a turtle counts as rushing–who is wincing as Carol helps move her. I maneuver myself around the old ladies and give Carol some counterbalance.

By the time we have Mom settled in her wheelchair, she's sweating.

"Mom," I ask, crouching down, "are you sure about this? I'm worried about you. You don't look like you're okay."

"I'm fine," she lies, giving me a very familiar smile. It's the smile that says she doesn't want to miss out on anything in life. My mother invented the fear of missing out. If she didn't already have a middle name, it should be FOMO.

"You're clearly in a lot of pain, Mom," Carol says, backing me up. We're both bent down now, on either side of her, and we're whispering. If we have any chance of convincing her to abandon this crazy outing, it's by staying quiet and close.

"I have to admit, this hurts more than I expected," Mom concedes, which is huge progress. You know that old Monty Python movie, the one with the knight who keeps getting his arms and legs chopped off and saying it's just a flesh wound?

My mother shares his DNA.

"Then how about we take you back ho–"

"Which is why I took some of those pain pills the doctor gave me."

Carol and I look at each other across Mom's lap.

"Some?" Carol asks. "How many?"

Mom waves a very loose hand. "I don't know. But I'm feeling better already."

A black sedan pulls into the parking area, moving with sharp pivots and a decisive style. The driver parks at the back of the small lot, choosing a spot as far as possible from any other cars.

On second look, it's an SUV, though a small one.

The driver's door opens and out steps Andrew, my brother-in-law's brother.

Then Declan, from the passenger seat. Oh, goody. Shannon convinced them to come, which means all the women in class are about to become a murmuration of starlings, telepathically communicating to their friends to get over to the yoga studio and watch the hot billionaires.

Then the door behind Andrew's opens and a very muscular leg, peppered with dark auburn hair, appears.

Followed by an ass.

Anatomically, that's impossible, yet in this case, it's very true. Hamish McCormick emerges from Andrew's car and looks toward the yoga studio, hands on his hips, an inquisitive smile turning his mouth into a small smirk.

"Mom," Carol says in a deeply amused voice, like her interest in this event just shot up three notches, "did you invite Hamish to this yoga class, too?"

"Hamish? Declan's Scottish cousin? No."

"Well, he's here."

"He is?" Mom is suddenly so relaxed, the words coming out in a pleasant, calm tone instead of her typical excited, over-the-top-shrieking response.

"Yep." Carol points to the three men, all now walking toward us. Declan looks at Mom in the wheelchair, eyes growing huge, brow moving down with concern.

Or calculation. My billionaire brother-in-law is not a stupid man. He fully understands the landscape here. Mom, at her best, is a tornado of activity, happiest when she's surrounded by noise, chaos, and constant busy-ness. The transfer of responsibility for Thanksgiving and this yoga class onto her daughters is bad enough.

Marie in a wheelchair, bored out of her mind, is bad news for everyone.

Agnes and Corrine are almost in the building when I see Agnes turn around, which is no small feat while clinging to a walker. It's as if she sensed Hamish, Declan, and Andrew, though they are hundreds of feet away and behind her.

"Where's your kilt?" she calls out. Hamish shakes his head at her.

"Ach, naw. Nae that one. She has an unhealthy obsession wi' kilts and ma stones."

Corrine waves sweetly at the men. Declan, with a tight smile, gives her a power wave, which means he lifts his arm exactly once, like he's catching a baseball, then drops it.

Meanwhile, being this close to Hamish has my skin tingling. Concentrating on keeping my breath steady takes all my energy. Regret fills me as I mentally survey my appearance.

Messy bun? Yep.

Didn't shower yet? Yep.

Hey, why bother when I'm about to get sweaty?

No makeup–hello? Putting on makeup for yoga is like washing your car before a thunderstorm. Sure, you can do it, but you're wasting your time.

Stop it, I tell my now self-conscious self. The world doesn't revolve around a tall, athletic ginger with an accent that melts panties.

Even my granny panties.

"Hello there, Amy," he says. "Carol."

"Hi," we say in unison.

"And Marie. Ach. What happened to yer leg?"

I look at him and shake my head furiously, slashing one finger across my neck. Is this a universal gesture? Do people in Scotland get it? I hope so. Listening to Mom describe the sex swing disaster again, and in front of Hamish, would be too much.

"My leg? I have legs?" Mom gasps.

"How many pain pills *did* you take?" Carol asks with alarm. She grabs the handles of Mom's wheelchair and starts guiding it toward the ramp, struggling to turn and steer.

"Allow me," Hamish insists, stepping in and moving the wheelchair with zero effort.

"I am so heavy," Mom mutters.

"Yer light as a feather, Marie," Hamish says graciously, giving me a wink.

He doesn't see the glare and frown I'm using to control his charms. Too bad I never went through a feminist witch phase like my friend Celine from high school. Now she works at one of those witchy stores in Salem and claims she taps into energy networks in other dimensions and times.

I wonder if she could sell me a spell to turn a Scotsman into a toad.

Or worse – into an Englishman.

The other women slowly making their way into the building have all frozen in place, pulling out phones, double-thumbing it on the glass. I know what this means. Shannon's described it before, and while I thought she was exaggerating, I'm seeing in real time that she wasn't.

The women are using their sisterhood network to call in their people.

Hot men at Marie's yoga class.

And just like that, Mom's broken leg turns into a community asset.

One tight ass at a time.

4

Hamish

A large group of women has its own scent.

And I love it.

Each woman is distinct, of course–especially in bed. For example, sporty women smell like salty, sweet sweat underneath the shampoo and perfume they use, their essence breaking through. That's how women are; the authenticity finds its way to the surface.

Which is how I know Amy is torn about me.

Never in my life have I pushed too hard with a woman. I'm not like that. If she wants me, she wants me. If she doesn't, I move on.

Amy, though... she drives me mad. Her signals don't add up. And when something doesn't add up, I can't let it go. Every action has a reason behind it. Part of being a top footballer is trusting your intuition. If you're too aware of your movements, you'll stumble. If you're not paying enough attention, you'll miss important cues.

The mind needs to be clear so the body can do what it instinctively needs to do.

You must trust yourself.

Which is why Amy's not making sense to me.

Why am I thinking about her so much, anyhow? She's no one to me. Just a girl to tease.

Most women are easier to charm. Maybe I just like the challenge.

I'm pushing Marie's wheelchair up a ramp to take her into this studio, which appears to be a renovated outbuilding and looks an awful lot like a chicken house, but that can't be right. It has wide, double glass doors in a red-painted frame, and natural grey shingles. Tiny windows run the length of the building. Declan, Andrew, Amy, and Carol are behind me, and behind them comes a flock of women.

Mind you, this is nothing new. I'm used to being followed by women in public, but not quite like this.

Because they're all on phones, and I can hear them telling friends to come to yoga.

"This is great," Marie says from her wheelchair. "The fire marshal is going to be so angry with me."

"Eh?"

"There's a capacity limit to the room. Last time we exceeded it was when Shannon met Declan and they started dating. She brought him to a class."

"How did ye get so many women to come?"

"I sent out a group text to my current students. We're a community. We care about each other. And part of caring is making sure we can all exploit every opportunity for eye candy."

"That sounds like ye're objectifying men's bodies, Marie."

"You sound like Amy when you talk like that! *Psssht*. We're just a bunch of fun-loving, vibrant women who do yoga so we don't throw our backs out when we put on a seatbelt. Give us our fun."

Just then, the older-than-dirt woman who likes to look up my kilt inches by, an oxygen tube up her nostrils. A young woman holding a small tank says something to her. I over-hear the words "grandma," "no cigarettes," and "yes, my generation is ruining everything."

"Hamish?"

Either I've gone silent, or Marie is high as a kite. Or both.

"Nae quarrel here, Marie. I think it's great. Life is meant to be filled with fun and laughter."

"Yes!" She tilts her head back and looks up at me, upside down. "You should date Amy."

"Excuse me?"

"Amy. My daughter."

"I know who she is, but why should I date her?"

Marie just blinks a wee bit, eyelids getting heavier. We're inside the building now, and Amy comes up and puts her hand on her mother's arm, about to ask her a question. Marie rouses and says:

"Because you'd make the most amazing little ginger babies together! Remember Hamy and Amy? How everyone matched up so nicely at Shannon and Declan's rehearsal dinner? Not Shannon and Declan, of course. No way to make those names rhyme. But Mandy and Andy. Carrie and Terry. Hamy and Amy!"

Amy's entire face opens with shock, accusing eyes meeting mine.

"What on Earth are you two talking about?"

"Sex," Marie replies.

"Of course you are. I wouldn't expect anything else from *you*." Amy pokes my chest with her index finger and inserts herself between me and her mother. "Where do you want to be, Mom?" she asks Marie, who is smiling like her lips are melting off her face.

"On stage."

The stage is a slightly elevated platform at the front of

the room. On it, my cousin Terry, who has a little more salt in his beard than last time we met, is moving a thin yoga mat into position. He's wearing tight workout leggings that end above his knee, a black knee band for patella support, and a wild tie-dye shirt that says he was born a generation too late.

Terry would have fit in very well in the 1960s.

Uncle James, when pissed, goes on about his oldest son. What a disappointment he is. How he walked away from everything. My role is to listen and let him rant; no one ever had to explain that to me. I know how it goes: Old alpha dogs gone to pasture expect the rest of us to listen to them growl at clouds.

But when I look at Terry, I see a man who knows himself. Would I have walked away from being a billionaire like he did? Don't know. Likely not. It's a big burden to take over a business your father built, but I know from experience that it's an even bigger weight on your shoulders to walk away from it.

Because I did the same.

No, you can't compare my Da's ice cream truck business to James's Fortune 500 behemoth, but the emotions are similar. Being a professional footballer softened the blow to Da, for sure. But it still hurt.

You torment yourself if you stay, and you let your father down if you leave.

No one wins.

That's why football is so much more appealing: There's always a winner.

And you do your damnedest to make sure it's you.

Ambiguity and football don't mix. You play and you play and you *play*, until one team emerges the victor, even if you have nothing left in you to give. You keep going because it's what you do. Not even because it's your job, you see. That fades fast.

It's who I am now. I just keep going, relentless and all in, until there's a winner.

And it better be me.

Feedback on the sound system buzzes loudly, forcing people to look up at Terry, who's adjusting the mic clipped to his t-shirt. I find my way to Declan and Andrew, who are surrounded by smiling women, some of them cutting their eyes over to Marie as if to say, *Why didn't you tell us they were coming?*

Clearly, not everyone got Marie's act-of-community-service group text.

A few are hastily bent over in the back of the room, compact mirrors pulled out, lipstick being applied like a peacock spreading its feathers, though that's the male putting on the display.

Speaking of strutting, where's Amy?

"Hamish," Andrew says. "Front row. Dec and I want to stare Terry down and make him screw up."

"Yer evil."

"No. Just brothers," Declan adds as they give each other a look I know all too well. I'm the oldest of my family, with too many little brothers and sisters. Da may be over seventy, but Mum is younger, and after me, they just kept going.

If one of *my* brothers were doing this yoga crap, we'd find a way to needle him, too.

I am taking my position in the front row, to the far left, Declan on my right, when Shannon and Amanda appear.

"Hamish! I didn't know you were in town!" Shannon says with a surprised jerk of her head when she sees me. As I reach down for a hug, I smell cardamom and coffee. Declan also broke away from James's company, buying a coffee chain with his wife, the two of them turning a few regional coffee shops into a national–and soon international–juggernaut.

I will welcome the day I can walk into a Grind It Fresh! shop in Glasgow or Edinburgh and enjoy an espresso that

originates with my cousin, but for now, I'm more than satis-
fied with The Milkman on Coburn Street.

Amanda comes in for a hug as well, her squeeze a bit
stronger than Shannon's.

"I am. Stuck here by your crazy holiday," I say as she pulls
away.

"Stuck?" Shannon asks, her head tilting as she asks, kind
eyes reminding me of Amy's, though a different color.

"Couldna get a flight home."

"Not a single seat?"

"Nae."

"Not even first class?"

My eyebrows go up and she laughs.

"Sorry. You'd think I'd know better. I'm getting spoiled
being married to him." She jerks her thumb toward Declan.

"It all works out. James offered me a job over the long
holiday."

"A job? Doing what?"

"Ach... an endorsement campaign. For Anterdec."

Amanda scowls. "I thought you were doing one for
Andrew's gyms."

"Aye. But James offered this to me as well. Work is work.
If I'm stuck here, might as well make money."

"That sucks to be stuck! Where are you staying?"
Shannon asks as Amanda busies herself with her yoga
equipment.

"Wi' James."

She flinches. "Oh, that's... wow. I'm so sorry." She looks at
Declan, who is walking toward us. "We have room if you
need another option."

I sling my arm around her shoulders and give her a
squeeze, laughing. "James is nothing compared to ma Da.
Getting along with cranky old men who are full of themselves
is ma superpower."

"I thought football was," Declan says.

"Being shallow is," Amy mutters under her breath as she walks past us.

I reach for her arm and gently hold her wrist. She halts, head tilting up, eyes a mix of emotions.

"Excuse me?" I ask, knowing damn well what she's just said.

"Your superpower is shallowness," she enunciates. "You're a mile wide and an inch deep."

"I assure ye, nothing on ma body is only an inch." I add a wink.

The beautiful rosy blush blooms on her upper chest and cheeks.

Tap tap tap

Another squeal of feedback follows Terry's finger tap on the microphone. "One minute, folks. Let's all find spots and get ready for some nice, relaxing fun."

"That's what Jerry used to say before we had sex," Agnes calls out. "Find your spot, Agnes, and get ready for some fun."

"GRANDMA!" the bonnie girl with her, dark haired and sharp, gasps.

The other old lady, next to the one with the oxygen, pats her blonde, feathered hair and says, "Oh, Cassie. That's nothing. If you can't handle Agnes at her porny best, how will you handle driving us all over kingdom come for your job?"

"Unemployment is starting to look good," the younger woman says softly.

"Hey! We just hired you. I'm your boss," Carol says to Cassie. "You can't quit. We'll never find anyone willing to work with those two." She points at Agnes and Corrine.

"Then you should pay Cassie more!" Agnes says with a cackle.

"Okay, everyone." Terry doesn't clap. Doesn't raise his deep voice. With a command I admire, he looks carefully into the crowd and smiles, people instantly giving him their attention. Jostling behind me ends with furious hisses, sounding something like a cat readying for a fight.

Then it goes quiet.

Amy

There's literally one spot left on the studio floor, way over on the left. As I roll out my mat and turn toward where Terry is standing on stage, I see an ass.

A really nice, muscular one.

I also see a different kind of ass.

Because it's *Hamish*.

Of all the people to end up behind, it has to be him.

And he has to be in *spectacular* shape.

Have you ever seen a person with a body part that is perfect? Not just perfect by your own standards, but objectively perfect? Greek-aesthetics perfect?

That's Hamish's ass.

Someone should sculpt it in marble.

He's wearing tight bike shorts, and as he turns in warrior pose, I see his inner thigh and think maybe I've gone to heaven without realizing it. If those main doors we walked through were the pearly gates, and this yoga studio is heaven, then I'm good.

Really.

I may not be particularly religious, but I *worship* men's soccer legs.

When I was younger, David Beckham's posters were all over my walls. Carol was partial to New Kids on the Block, but give me Posh Spice's husband any day.

That fine, fine butt.

With Hamish facing forward, I can get an eyeful without

being obvious, which means I'm now filled with an unbearably complicated set of feelings.

Feelings, unlike operational tasks, cannot be added to a spreadsheet, color-coded, prioritized, and checked off my to-do list. Being here at this yoga class is killing me, and not just because I'm imagining Hamish under silk sheets and me under Hamish.

Oh, no.

Because I have an enormous project to manage with the undertaking of Thanksgiving, and being at this stupid ninety-minute yoga class, with forty-two minutes of driving included in the time block, is taking precious time away from what I do best:

Optimize.

Nothing about Hamish is optimal. He inserts himself into moments in my life when all he does is distract. *Sub*tract. Make a situation worse.

Make me perform at my worst.

He's like Mom, but in hot athletic form. There is no simple situation Marie Jacoby cannot twist into a multi-layered, backtracking mess that takes twice as long and three times the resources to complete.

Hamish does the same thing to my emotions.

The Thanksgiving debacle does have a silver lining, though.

I spent half the night taking the chaos of Mom's broken leg and turning it into a shining example of how efficiency can triumph.

But we have to be home in exactly one-hundred and eighteen minutes for the rest of the day to go smoothly, so tomorrow, Carol, Shannon, Dad, and I can prove to Mom that we're better at Thanksgiving than she is.

"Restorative yoga isn't like regular yoga," Terry explains, breaking through my thoughts. I tear my eyes away from Hamish's butt and give Terry my full attention.

Which is considerable, given how much of it I was giving to Hamish.

"You'll notice that at the end of each row, there are extra yoga blocks and blankets. Please make sure you have two blocks and as many blankets as you need to be warm. We'll do some slow breathing exercises, a few long, warm stretches, and then we'll redistribute around the edges of the room for some poses up against the wall."

"I like it up against the wall. Great leverage," I hear Hamish whisper as he gives a purple yoga block a hard squeeze. Shannon snorts and gives him a sassy look as I turn green inside and nearly explode.

No, Shannon isn't flirting with him. That's not what makes me jealous. It's the easy way she can joke with him, casual and lighthearted.

Why does it bother me so much? He's a cad and a jerk. I shouldn't even want to be able to joke with him like my sister can.

And yet...

Soft Buddhist music, full of low chimes, fills the air. Terry walks over to a panel on the edge of the stage and turns the lights way down, earning an "Oooooh" from Mom, who is tucked away in her wheelchair, leg sticking out like a white plaster erection, in a corner by the three steps leading up to the stage. As the lights dim, a series of small, glowing, white lotus-shaped lamps gives the room a gauzy feel.

My shoulders drop. Warmth fills my back, and I take a deep breath without even trying.

Terry is encouraging us to reach up, stretching from the base of the spine. My eyes adjust to the changing light and continue to catalog Hamish's body. His shorts are so tight, I can see the double chain of muscles along his back. He's a marvelous specimen of the masculine ideal: tall, thickly muscular, with an athleticism and grace that frankly *should* be monetized.

He's been naked on sports magazine covers. Done endorsements for regional breweries and energy bars. I know from Declan that he's close to making it big.

He's *already* big.

My eyes dart to his feet.

How big *is* he?

Heat fills me at the thought, a combination of self-loathing and desire. Which is nothing new for me when it comes to Hamish McCormick.

Why did he have to be here? Now? Of all times, when Mom has a broken leg and we're already in disarray? I'm finally finishing my MBA, working another co-op at a venture capital firm. My last one was disrupted by scandal after the high-profile associate gunning for partner turned out to be married to a massive conman. I think I might have gotten my new co-op just for my potential gossip supply.

But my life is smoothing out now. It took me eight years to earn my bachelor's, but with Declan's help, the MBA has been full time, which is *so* much easier. I've told him straight out I don't want any favors, and I refuse to work for Grind It Fresh! Or Anterdec. No nepotism.

Though I'll certainly network and accept help making connections.

I'm on the cusp of a new life, moving into adulthood at last. I finished a major project yesterday, excited for the Thanksgiving break. I was at the gym, fresh off submitting my group work to our professor, when Dad called about the –

Well. You know.

And now Mom and Dad broke her leg and half their bedroom, my sisters and I have to manage Thanksgiving dinner from scratch, and I can't stop ogling Hamish's ass.

That's too much input.

"Let go of troubling thoughts," Terry says in soothing, deep dulcet tones as we do triangle pose, our breathing syncing with slow movement. Hamish's arms stretch out and down. He has muscles on top of muscles, with fine ginger hair all over his arms, darkening as it tapers to his wrists. When we all go into a partial squat, his hamstrings pop like cello strings under his skin, each tiny muscle and tendon in stark relief across a body I could watch forever.

Too bad he has the emotional maturity of a hedgehog.

And that might be giving him too much credit.

"Fine form," Hamish whispers to Shannon, who blinks fast.

"Thanks. I've been doing yoga on my lunch breaks. Even fifteen minutes makes a difference."

"Aye. People think it's about doing long workouts but smaller amounts of time really do add up."

Insane–they're driving me insane. How can they just idly chat like that while every inch of my skin is on fire? Every breath turns into a proto-orgasm as I watch him stealthily.

Or maybe not stealthily enough. He turns around, catches me watching, and winks.

Damn it.

I hate this. I hate reacting to him like this. I hate that he knows he's doing this to me, and he revels in it. I *hate* that he's so smarmy and overconfident and...

Tantalizing.

I'm going to assume that when all the blood in my body rushes to the surface of my skin and between my legs, it means my IQ drops a bit; lack of oxygen to the brain is the only explanation I have for finding him so attractive. This is a purely physiological response, driven entirely by evolution.

This is not my fault.

He's big and strong, and his physicality signals virility and protection. Biology is an amazing science, its processes optimized to drive us to reproduce.

My blushing, my throbbing, the zings running across my arms and legs–it's just electrical impulses, a response shaped over hundreds of thousands of years to produce the right outcome: hot, sweaty, reproductive sex.

Penis-in-vagina sex.

Eggs in a sperm bath.

Sperm with determination to crack open that outer shell and wiggle on in.

It's really just that simple.

I don't emotionally desire this guy. Not one little bit. My heart isn't attracted to Hamish McCormick.

My eggs are.

Bad ova. Bad, *bad* ova.

As Terry guides us into standing forward bend, Hamish doubles over, and my urge to moan at the vision before me is tempered only by biting my lower lip.

His green eyes meet mine, upside down and through his legs. His grin is disconcerting, warm and flirty as he says, "Enjoying the view?"

"*Shhh.*"

"Ye keep eyeing me like I'm a big, juicy steak, Amy. Wondering what I taste like? If so, the feeling's mutual."

"You are such a pig."

"Ye started it, objectifying me."

"I objectified you? You are so full of yourself. How is it possible to objectify someone who sat naked on a soccer goal on the front cover of *Sports Illustrated*?"

"Ye saw that, did ye?"

"Of course I did. You couldn't miss it. It was in every grocery store checkout line!"

"And ye bought a copy, aye?"

"*Shhh.*" Declan shoots us both a miffed look. "We're trying to do yoga here."

Andrew snorts. "You're making weird faces at Terry, trying to throw him off his game."

"And it's not going to work if these two keep flirting. Their whispering is distracting."

"FLIRTING?" I snap, louder than I wanted to. "I am *not* flirting with him!"

Andrew snorts even louder. Terry looks in our direction and frowns.

"Trade places wi' me, Amy. Fair is fair. I need equal time to stare at *yer* arse," Hamish purrs. Purrs! He sounds like a Scottish Chuckles.

"My ass has nothing to do with this!"

"Oh, I beg to differ."

"Don't bring my ass into this, Hamish! You leave my ass alone!"

Suddenly, the room is dead quiet.

"I told you we picked the wrong side of the room to be on, Agnes," Corrine says loudly. "There's ass play going on over there."

"Well, how was I supposed to know? Besides, there isn't a plug over there for my oxygen concentrator. Someone let the battery run down before we got here," Agnes replies, glaring at her granddaughter.

"'Someone' is you, Grandma. I'm not your battery minder," Cassie replies with a meaningful throat clearing that makes it obvious they are related.

Corrine whacks Agnes on the arm. "Breathe harder, Agnes. We're missing out on the good life over there. They're talking about anal!"

There are moments in life when you want a *deus ex machina* to appear. A god in the machine to swoop in and save you. I learned about this Greek theater concept in the eleventh grade, and I still thank my English teacher for making us pronounce it properly (even docking points on our final grade if we got it wrong).

Anyway, it turns out to be real.

Because at that exact moment–Corrine's final word ringing loud and clear, Terry looking over at us from the stage with his eyebrows raised, Buddhist monks chanting between long, deep gong tones–the fire alarm begins its own deep, piercing tone.

Terry's head jerks up, looking for the exits. Red lights are flashing. The women in the back start rolling their mats up, some just dragging them, juggling water bottles and half-filled gym bags, finding coats at the row of hooks near the entrance, shoving bare feet into boots and shuffling outside.

New Englanders are nothing if not practical when it comes to the cold and snow.

"Smoke," Hamish shouts, pointing to the right of the stage. Sure enough, I see it before I smell it, a small, steady stream of grey ribbons pouring out from somewhere down the hallway. The sight fills me with fear.

Pandemonium breaks out as the sound of the alarm disorients everyone. I'm pressing my fingers against my tragus, closing my ears as much as possible, scanning the room.

"MOM!" Carol shouts, racing to her.

Hamish is next to me, big hand going to my shoulder as he bends down and looks me in the eye.

"Amy, get out!"

"My mom!" I scream back. "Wheelchair!"

Those green eyes change, darting for a split second, calculating.

Then he acts.

When a soccer player runs for the ball, he is single-threaded, fully focused on using situational awareness and muscle memory to accomplish a quickly envisioned goal, distilling tens of thousands of hours of practice into a pin-point moment.

Hamish does the same thing to rescue my mother.

He's at her chair in seconds, sliding one arm under her thick cast, urging her hands around his neck with a nonverbal grace I can't admire right now, because pure panic is shooting through me.

Then I see Cassie unplugging Agnes's oxygen pack and realize we have more than just my mom to worry about.

"Andrew!" Declan bellows, the two racing over to Agnes and Corrine, each one scooping an old woman in their arms.

Corrine's face turns into a sun, her joy so out of step with the horror of what's happening.

And then the sprinklers kick in.

Instead of running, Hamish walks carefully, Mom moaning in pain with each step. I'm right next to them. Carol is pushing Mom's wheelchair, and Shannon is helping Declan and Cassie with Agnes's oxygen. Most of the students have left, and Terry stands by the door, calm but sharp, waving people out while counting.

"Carol?" he calls out in a deep voice, scanning the room.

"Here!" she calls out from behind Mom's empty wheelchair. As a cluster of people make it past him, Carol in his line of sight now. Terry nods, eyes softening a bit, but he continues counting, clearly in charge.

"Get out of here," Declan growls at him as he walks by carrying Agnes, who looks like she's on an amusement park ride and Declan is her roller coaster seat. The spray of sprinkler water adds to the illusion, as if we've just gotten off a different ride, a mock whitewater rapids, only indoors.

Shannon holds the door for the three men as they exit. She pats my shoulder and we just nod at each other, eyes big as the wet hair mats around our faces. We look like Mom's dog, Chuffy, during a bath in the kitchen sink, all eyes and clumps of flat hair.

And fear.

Cheers greet me as I walk outside, but they're not cheering for me. A fire truck is pulling in, the sound of women clapping and hooraying immediately overwhelmed by the sirens.

Cameras face the three McCormick men, each carrying a damsel in distress.

"My hair!" Corrine shrieks.

I take a step toward her and realize my feet are bare, the cold shooting through me instantly. The shock of escaping the burning building is receding enough to realize my mistake.

And then I feel fur. *Wet* fur.

Wet, cold fur.

"You're stepping on Petunia!" Corrine screams at me as I leap back, the tiny animal smooshed into the snow. What have I done?

"I'm so sorry!" I bend down, my feet sinking deeper into the snowbank, tentatively poking the little creature. It doesn't move. Did I kill it? It feels too cold to have just now stepped on it and crushed it.

"Petunia," Corrine wails. "My favorite!"

Oh, no. I've read that old people can become extremely attached to pets, needing the companionship. My heart sinks and as the sirens blare around us, my eyes assaulted by the flash of red and white lights, I start to feel dizzy.

Then Cassie marches over, feet encased in boots like a normal person, and bends down, snatching up the poor pet's body.

She holds it out, shaking it hard. I suppress a scream.

Until I realize what it really is.

A wig.

I've been poking a *wig*. Feeling bad for a *wig*.

Cassie's eyes meet mine.

"Want a job? Because I'm pretty close to quitting."

"God, no." I point to my mother. "I'll be taking care of her in twenty years. You're my future."

Cassie half laughs, half cries. "Good luck."

Hamish settles Mom into her wheelchair. His wet workout clothes are even tighter and his ginger waves, now deep rust, are plastered against his skin. Somehow, as we exited, he managed to get his feet into his shoes.

Suddenly, I'm in the air, staring at clouds, confused. My face is wet, pressed against a deep, hard warmth that smells like sweat and wet cotton.

"What are you doing?"

"Saving yer feet. Ye dinna get yer shoes?"

"I wasn't paying attention." Tears fill my eyes. The fire-fighters are entering the building in their gear, and the reality of what just happened is sinking in. Most of the yoga students are now huddled in their cars, a few already pulling out of the parking lot.

"Where do ye need to go? Which car?" he asks, looking down at me with such a tender expression, it just makes me cry even more, my throat too tight for words.

All I can do is point to Carol, Mom, and Shannon, now gathered next to our minivan.

Hamish is strong, but I'm not exactly a small woman. The press of his forearm under my knees and the way his fingers under my shoulders brush against the side of my breast make me pull even closer to him, tightening my arms around his neck. He smells good. So, so good.

And he's so big and hard. How can skin be so taut? Every piece of him has a specific purpose, precisely carved.

"Yer shivering."

The warmth of his breath against my cheek gives me life. His body is a breathing hot pack.

Hot *eight*-pack.

"Amy!" Shannon dashes over with a mylar bivouac Dad keeps in the back of the car for emergencies.

This moment definitely qualifies.

Shannon covers me with the silver sleeping bag, tucking an edge in under Hamish's hand.

"Get her in the car," Carol urges. Shannon opens the front passenger-side door and Hamish crouches, sliding me easily into the seat, still covered with the blanket. Coordination is his strong suit.

So are those incredible thighs.

"Amy," he says seriously, smoothing the blanket over my feet.

"I'm fine. No need to fuss over me. I just got stupid in there and forgot my shoes."

"I'll turn on the car and get the heat going!" Carol calls out as more fire trucks appear, and the sound of a news helicopter makes us all look up.

Mary Elizabeth, Mom's friend who owns the former chicken coop/yoga torture studio, tears into the parking lot in her silvery-blue Mercedes SUV. She rents the place out to people like my mom for classes and events, but she's always been very hands off. She slams on the brakes, not bothering to park within the painted lines, and jumps out of the car, her red coat unzipped and her body language rife with panic.

"MARIE?" she screams across the lot, hands in her hair. "Are you okay? What happened?"

Carol rolls down Mom's window.

"I don't know! Smoke started pouring out from the hallway where the bathrooms are." She points to Hamish and looks around, finding Declan and Andrew talking to firefighters. "Hamish carried me out."

Mary Elizabeth screws up her face in confusion. "Hamish?"

"Aye. That'd be me."

A painfully slow turn of her head, toward his voice and then up, up, up to catch his eye, makes my cold, shivering self pay attention.

"Well, hello there," she says in a low, caramel voice. "If my barn had to catch on fire, it was worth it to meet *you*." She steps forward and offers her hand. "Thank you so much for helping. Are you a student of Marie's? She didn't tell me she's recruiting *Sports Illustrated* covers in human form."

Someone as full of themselves as Hamish should be flattered by her comment. Should join in jocular banter. Should go into full flirt mode, even though she's older than my mother.

I start to disengage from the conversation, body struggling to fight its way out of mild shock and the cold. The open window on Mom's side is rendering the van's heater useless.

But instead of taking Mary Elizabeth's comments as confirmation that he's a gift to the world, Hamish's brows crowd each other, nose wrinkling slightly in what looks like... anger?

"Fer God's sake, woman, yer barn just caught fire with thirty people in it. Quit wasting yer time talking to me and go deal with the firemen."

Astonishment makes her face go blank for a moment, then she reddens, turns away, and jogs over to one of the firefighters.

"That was harsh," Carol says, nodding with approval.

"The woman was flirtin' wi' me in the middle of a fire."

"Right?" Carol agrees. "Who does that?"

"Lots of 'em," he sighs. "I was once on a crowded train and some poor sod had a seizure. A group of us tried to help him and in the middle of it, his wife slipped me her number. Tiny piece o' paper into ma back pocket."

"What?" Carol quirks one eyebrow.

"Aye. Women are strange."

"Hamish?" Mom says from the backseat. "What're you doing for Thanksgiving?"

"Whatever Uncle James is doing."

"Oh!" Mom brightens. "Goody. Then we'll see you tomorrow."

"Aye?"

"You're coming to our house with James, right."

"Looking forward to it, Marie."

My stomach drops. Carol, Shannon, and I have our work cut out for us, preparing everything for tomorrow's feast. A huge grocery order's being delivered right now, Dad nicely offering to put everything away. We bought pre-made pies, and the turkey's in the fridge. Since it's a fresh one from a local farm, we don't have to worry about defrosting.

Working hard to pull off the holiday doesn't bother me, though it was unexpected.

Add Hamish to the mix?

I'm bothered, all right.

Hot and bothered.

For some reason, I yawn. Maybe it's my body's way of pushing oxygen into my blood so my brain stays sharper and prevents me from doing something foolish.

Like taking Hamish up on his offers.

"Poor Amy. The fire took a lot out o' ye."

"No. I'm just bored hearing you preen about how every hetero woman wants to sleep with you."

He winks. "And some o' the lesbians."

"You can't be human for more than two minutes straight, can you? You're a two-minute man. A less-than-two-minute man."

That offends him. "Take that back. No' true a'tall."

"I will not take it back!"

He winks. "I last far longer than two minutes. Give me a chance and I'll show ye."

"See? Two minutes. You go from kind and compassionate and protective to slimy and vulgar in a hundred and twenty seconds."

"I think yer just jealous o' that woman, the owner."

"WHAT?"

"Ye dinna like it when other women eye me, Amy."

"Shut up. Carol, let's get out of here. I'm shivering."

"Wi' lust."

"You ruin everything, Hamish! You pig!"

As Carol moves the car forward, he laughs. The sound makes my heart hurt, even as my feet are warming up, tingling painfully, parts waking up to the pain of discovery and the relief of being okay.

I watch Hamish run over to his cousins, still chatting with the firefighters and now joined by Mary Elizabeth.

"Shannon left. Had to get home to Ellie," Carol tells me. "What about your shoes?"

"They're probably soaked back there. I'll get them another day. Let's just go home."

She gives me curious side eye. "Okay. And what's up with you and Hamish?"

"Nothing."

"That didn't sound like nothing."

"He's an empty flirt who is gorgeous and he knows it, which makes him far less attractive."

"'Less attractive' and 'Hamish' don't go in the same sentence."

"There's way more to being attractive than just looks!"

"Like your father," Mom mumbles from the back seat. "He's not classically good looking, but lordy, that man has a tongue designed by the devil that takes me straight to heaven."

"MOM!" we both scream. Carol swerves on the road, nearly hitting a snowbank.

"Don't do that to me when I'm driving!" she snaps at Mom. "And you, Amy. Don't fight it. Sleep with Hamish."

"I don't want to sleep with Hamish!"

Mom and Carol snort so loudly, they sound like a camel caravan. I'm half expecting the spitting to start next.

"I don't want to sleep with Hamish because I have no desire to be a notch on his belt."

"I wonder what they use in Scotland for the notching," Mom asks dreamily.

"You know what I mean."

"Sounds like you want more than just a good lay out of him," Carol says slowly, eyeing me with care.

"What? No!"

"Bet he's great in bed."

"That has nothing to do with this."

"Doesn't it? The whole point of guys like Hamish is to sleep with them. Enjoy it. Keep it as a lovely memory to draw on when life gets overwhelming or boring and routine."

"I'm not that shallow."

"Maybe you need to let someone shallow get a little deep into you, Amy."

"That makes no sense, Mom."

"Neither does turning Hamish down."

"Just because he's conventionally gorgeous, has a smoking hot body, is an increasingly famous athlete, and keeps coming on to me doesn't mean I should sleep with him!"

Carol pulls the car over, slamming it into park. As she turns on me, I have flashbacks of summer vacation road trips, Dad twisting around in the seat, yelling at us that he'll turn the car around if we don't cut it out.

"What are your standards, Amy? Holding out for a prince? Because Meghan Markle already got him."

"I don't like Hamish, okay?"

"Your blood sure does," Mom says with a cackle. "Look at that blush. You're just like Jason."

She's right, and I hate that she's right. Dad has the same flushing thing. Being a redhead sucks.

"I don't have to justify why I don't want to sleep with him. I can't believe you're teasing me for *not* having sex with the guy."

"We're not teasing you for your choice," Carol says as she eases back onto the road. "We're teasing you because you're deluding yourself."

"Huh?"

"If you don't like Hamish, that's a fine reason not to screw him. But it's clear as day that you *do* want to screw him."

"I can't stand him!"

"Doesn't mean you don't want a rousing round of hate sex."

"Hate sex? What is that?"

Mom says the phrase, only she uses the f-word instead of sex.

"Those are great," Mom says softly. "You get into a big fight and then you just pound it all out."

"You two are gross."

"But we're not wrong. You're holding yourself back from testing the waters with him," Carol says.

"I am holding myself back from getting an antibiotic-resistant STD from him."

"Keep telling yourself that, Amy."

"Besides, I am too busy for a relationship."

Carol giggles. "Hamish isn't offering you a relationship. He's renting you his todger for a night."

"Ewww!"

"Can you do that?" Mom says with a yawn. "Rent them? Like going to the hardware store and renting a post-hole digger for a day?"

"He'll drill nice and deep into your lawn, Amy," Carol says with a snicker.

"SHUT UP!"

I give them the silent treatment the rest of the way home.

And torture myself with recalling every moment in Hamish's arms.

5

Hamish

I 've been to the Jacoby's a number of times before, but I've never walked in to find a giant dead chicken on the kitchen counter, with Amy's hand so far up its arse, it's like she's giving it a prostate exam.

"Careful. Ye touch the right spot and he'll give ye a pearl necklace," I joke as I set a half-case of wine on a different counter, along with a bag holding a small container of saffron, a mesh bag of shallots, and a hostess gift. The house smells like sautéed onions and yeasty bread, with a strong sage and thyme component to it. Unlike James's house, the Jacoby residence is a home. Lived in and filled with people bonded to each other, with worn edges to objects.

And few edges on people.

Amy's mouth forms an O of surprise. "This is its head, not its ass!"

"What're you doing to the poor carcass?"

"Massaging olive oil into the inside before we put the stuffing in."

"How big is that chicken?"

"It's a turkey. And it's twenty-four pounds. Why are you here so early? It's 9 a.m.!"

"Don't ask me, I'm just following orders. James had his driver bring me because yer mum needed these." I pick up the shallots and saffron, shaking them.

"When is James coming?"

"In his words, 'at a civilized two p.m.'"

"So you're here for five hours before everyone else comes?"

"Aye. But I plan to go out fer a run." I give her a look. "Brought ma workout clothes. Marie said it was fine."

She turns red. "Whatever you say."

"I hear ye run, too."

"I do."

"Want to run wi' me?"

"What? No."

"Why no'? Runners are runners."

A strange look passes over her face, one of longing. "I wish I could," she says in a tone of confession. "Truly. But I'm too busy."

"Another time, then?"

"If it's just running, then yes."

"What's that supposed to mean, Amy?"

"You keep hitting on me."

"I do?"

"Don't do that, Hamish. Don't play that game. You know you're doing it."

"I'm flirting."

"You're fishing."

"Same thing."

"No, it's not. And it makes me uncomfortable."

"Good."

"Good?"

"Life isn't about being comfortable all the time. The discomfort is where the good stuff happens. Ye learn about yerself. Pieces of ye that would stay hidden otherwise get exposed to some light and seen. What're ye hiding in yer own shadows?"

"That's remarkably philosophical for a guy who called me at three a.m. to ask me which shades of pink my labia are."

"I did?"

"Yes. And you asked if the carpet matches the drapes. Then you paused, and asked if I even had a carpet, and mused that it might be a landing strip, or a bare wood floor, or – "

"I wouldna do such a thing!"

"You absolutely did."

I reach for her hair, a lock escaping her messy bun. "Yer a natural redhead. I am as well. I would never."

"Then you were deeper in your cups on that call than you realized."

"If there's one thing a Scotsman can do, it's hold his liquor. I wasna *that* pissed."

"Keep telling yourself that, tough guy." She frowns, lightly caressing the outside of the turkey, finally done violating it. Latex gloves cover her hands, and a flash of her in a nurse's uniform, with garters and white high heels, makes my blood pulse, skin going tight.

It's going to be a long holiday.

The oven beeps and we both turn, just as Carol walks into the kitchen. She comes to a screeching halt, unbalanced on her heels. The oldest of the Jacoby sisters, she looks the most like her mother. Sounds like her mother.

But is nothing like her.

"Hamish! You're early!" Her hand goes to her hair, finger combing it.

"Aye, Marie told me to come. Dinna worry, I'll be out o' yer way shortly. Going fer a run."

"A run? Amy runs. Why don't you go together?"

"Because I have a holiday dinner to cook," Amy replies through gritted teeth, fingering a stack of printouts. Looks suspiciously like color-coded financial reports my agent is constantly looking through when we meet.

"A run could do you some good. Release some endorphins. You've got plenty of those pent up, Ames. Wouldn't want to explode now, would you?"

"Shut up."

"Ach," I mutter. "I'm feeling like I'm back home."

"What's that supposed to mean?" she snaps.

"Americans are too friendly. Too cheery and fake. When ye snap and tease each other like this, it's like we're back in ma kitchen at home."

"You're a weird man, Hamish. You enjoy conflict?" Carol says in that smooth voice of hers.

"I enjoy people who are real."

"Says the cocky jerk who wouldn't know depth if he fell down a mine shaft," Amy replies.

"Thinking about shafts, are you?" Carol responds.

Amy's eyes close, lips forming a thin line as her throat bobs with a swallow. She picks up the enormous roasting pan with the turkey and moves it closer to the oven.

"Lemme help ye," I insist, laughing inside as Carol chortles. The oven's hot, so I open the door as Amy hefts the big, oiled-up beastie and aims it for the rack.

But...

"It doesn't fit!" Amy moans, the top two inches of the turkey looking like the top of a lorry caught in the arch of a railway trestle.

"It *always* fits," Carol says, sounding puzzled, as they analyze the situation.

"I can't hold this position! I'm getting a cramp," Amy complains.

Carol tilts her head, studying the physics of it. "We need more oil. It'll fit if we angle it just so and make sure everything's nice and slick."

"If we rub it some more and press down a little, that might work."

"But not too much! Then it'll be done too fast and we don't want that. We need plenty of time for it to get nice and juicy." Amy pauses, breathing hard. "I can't hold this position!"

"What if we lift one leg like this," Carol says, biting her lower lip. "And you put your hand here."

Amy makes a sound of satisfaction. "Ahhhhh. My cramp's gone. That feels *so* much better!"

I swear she moans.

Carol starts giving the turkey little pats that apply more and more pressure. I half expect it to pinken and beg for another.

"I never knew Thanksgiving could be so arousing," I comment. Carol's face goes blank, then reddens, a curling smile turning to giggles.

Amy lets out an aggrieved sigh. "Only *you* could make roasting a turkey into something porny."

"Ye're the one moaning about positions and cramps and oil!"

"What's this I hear? Are you talking about porn?" Marie calls out from the living room.

"That's Mom's bat signal," Carol mutters.

"Hamish?" Marie's voice is high with inquiry. Or pain killers. I can't quite tell which. "Is that you?"

"Aye, Marie."

"Did you bring the shallots and saffron?"

"Of course. And Cousin James sent half a case o' wine as well."

No one told me the appropriate hostess gift for a day when you hunt down a big, dumb bird that roams the woods of New England, kill and dress it, roast it, and invite your friends over to *ooooh* and *ahhhh* at the size of it.

So I improvised.

I pick up the gift and walk to the living room.

"And this is for ye, Marie. I wasna going to give it now, but why no'?" The tiny silver and red foil package weighs nothing in my hand. Marie picks it up. The whole family is so casual, wearing pajamas and baffies, hair messy, and moving with an air of calm busyness. The warm scent of spices hints at the feast to come, and I feel a growing satisfaction.

Today will be a good day.

"Jason!" Marie bellows, blasting through the calm, the cat spitting and hissing, the dog jumping up from his little bed, tail wagging as he finds my foot and gives it a good hump.

Chuffy.

She named the wee bastard after a bum. I'll never get over it.

Amy's father, Jason, walks in. His hair is corkscrewing like auburn fire, greying and balding at the edges. Friendly blue eyes meet mine, and I'm struck a bit.

He could blend right in with Mum's side of the family.

The man's wearing a faded concert t-shirt with a Goth band on it, flannel pajama pants, and red baffies with tufts of stuffing poking out at the little toe of one foot.

A friendly hand comes out for a shake.

"You're early," he says, making me laugh.

"Blame yer wife. It was a saffron emergency."

"Thank you for saving us from certain doom, then. I owe you my life. Three hundred years ago, I'd owe you a daughter."

He winks.

I don't.

"Oh, stop it, Jason," Marie says, batting him with the back

of one hand. "Look what Hamish brought us!" She holds the gift aloft.

"It's nothing. A wee thank ye." I glance at the big grandfather clock near their piano. "And I'll be out o' yer hair shortly. I have a few hours of training to do."

"You brought a change of clothes, I hope? Feel free to shower and get ready for dinner here," Marie says with a half smile.

"Aye, I did. Thank ye. Running on the streets of Boston isn't quite as good as a wide-open trail run."

"Boston proper has plenty of trails," Amy shouts from the kitchen.

"No' the same when ye can hear the lorries and cars. At home, I like to bag a Munro fer fun, but I'll settle fer a nice rail trail here."

"Bag a what?" Amy says, coming out of the kitchen, wrangling her hair back up and wrapping a hair tie around the wild wonder of it.

"Munro."

"You cannot have a conversation without mentioning sex, can you? You're just like my mother."

"HEY!" Marie and I call out at the same time.

"And what does it mean, what I said?" I challenge her.

"Bagging someone is slang for having sex with them."

"Ach. Nae. Even I canna bag a Munro like that. In Scotland, it means to climb a small mountain."

"Oh."

"See, Amy?" Carol says as she comes into the living room, wiping her hands on a kitchen towel. "You don't know everything."

"I never said I did."

"And Hamish isn't the only one who thinks about sex all the time."

"I do not!"

"How about we open Hamish's gift?" Jason says diplomatically, clearly accustomed to keeping the peace in this family. Seems like a full-time job.

"Ye dinna have to open it in front o' everyone," I say, though I shoot Amy a grin, delighted she's here. "It's just a little something. Meant more as a laugh to be shared than anything practical."

"So it's a metaphor for you?" Amy says with a smirk.

Ouch.

"Condoms?" Marie asks as she opens the wrapping.

Amy's face sours. "I was right," she says with a snort.

"Wine condoms," I correct Marie. "Read the label."

Jason pulls the small box out and holds it aloft. "He isn't kidding. Wine condoms."

"Perfect!" Marie claps. "Chuffy chewed both of our bottle stoppers a few weeks ago, and I had it on my list to get new ones, but these are better. You just roll it on the shaft and never have to worry again!"

Jason bursts out laughing. "But what if it breaks? Then everything's ruined."

Marie pulls a gold-foil packet out of the box, tearing it open with her hand and teeth like a pro.

"Nice," she mumbles. "No lube. I hate how that bit of lube gets on your tongue when you're opening one."

"Can we open a bottle of that wine *now*?" Carol asks, cutting me a look. "I need a glass to get through this conversation."

"Jason, get a bottle of wine," Marie orders, the man moving like a pack animal whose spirit was broken long ago.

Carol perks up. "It's only 9:30, but hey. Tough times call for tough measures."

I laugh. These people do remind me of my own family back home. It's nice. America is a strange and brutal land; so many people smiling to my face then stabbing me in the back with knives they keep well hidden. The Jacoby family is real.

I like real.

Fake America pays my bills, though. Endorsements for products that companies sell to the public by convincing them that their life will be better with a sports towel, an electrolyte solution, or a cream—that's where much of my money comes from.

Money that makes life easier for the folks back home.

Jason brings in an open bottle of merlot, reaches for the condom in Marie's hand, and deftly smoothes the black, unlubricated condom over the neck.

"Nice technique," I say to him.

He blushes, a twin to Amy.

"Uh... thanks?"

"Can we move on from all this condom talk?" Amy grouses.

"Ye need to get back to shoving yer hand up a bird's arse?"

"Neck. That's the neck. How many times have I told you? And Carol and I got the turkey in the oven, thank you. Now it spends hours roasting."

"So ye're done? Ye get to rest and relax?"

Marie, Carol, and Amy all burst out into braying laughter, like I've unleashed a pack of hyenas.

"Hamish," Jason says quietly, taking my elbow. "Let me show you my den."

"Den?"

"We need to get out of here," he whispers as I lean down to hear him, "before they stop laughing."

"Why?"

A yank of my arm is all I get for an answer. Jason leads me through their kitchen, past the table, and out the sliding glass door into a back yard covered in brown grass.

"There's my smoker," he says proudly, pointing to a big black contraption that looks like a barrel on its side. It's definitely seen better days. "That's where I smoked the turkey."

"But the turkey's in the oven."

"We're doing two, one roasted, one smoked. Some people prefer one over the other. Plus, we want to be sure there's plenty to go around."

"How did ye smoke it?"

"First, I rubbed it with garlic and butter. Then I mixed up spices and Coca Cola, and poured that over. And then I basted it every hour for ten hours, and checked the temperature till it got to 180 degrees."

"Sounds like a great deal o' work. Ye cook the bird fer ten hours and everyone's finished eating it in twenty minutes."

"I stayed up most of the night, but when you taste the meat, you'll understand."

"I'm impressed. That kind of effort means it must be important."

He eyes me for a second longer than needed, smiling.

At the far end of the yard is a small shed. He opens the door, revealing a single room furnished with a brown upholstered recliner, another big chair, a television on a stand, a mini fridge like you find in hotel rooms, some tools, and a small electric heater, which he turns on.

"What's this?"

"My man cave."

"It's no' so much a cave as a utility closet wi' a telly."

"It's my space. The women leave me alone here."

"Ooooh. Got it. Da uses the water heater room in the cellar to hide his porno magazines and smoke in secret."

"I guess this is my version of that." He looks at the fridge. "Normally, I'd offer a beer, but it's 9:30 in the morning."

"It's 2:30 in the afternoon back in Glasgow," I offer.

Hearty laughter pours forth as he has a seat, gesturing for me to do the same. "Let's stay in here until they get busy again."

"Shouldn't we help?"

"Oh, we'll be helping all day. And I heard you tell Marie you need to go for a run?"

"Right. A long run, and then some sprints."

"You do that all the time?"

"Every day."

"As part of your job?"

"Aye. Footballers have to stay in top shape."

"Do you like it?"

"The training? Nae. But ye do it anyhow."

"Football. Being a football player. Do you like it?"

What a question. No one's ever asked me that before.

"Of course I do!" I answer with gusto. "I'd be insane no' to!"

"Why?"

"Because it's every lad's dream."

"Just because it's every lad's dream doesn't mean it makes *you* happy."

I think I'd rather take my chances with the hyena women in the house than have my psyche plumbed out here.

"What about ye, Jason? Are ye happy in yer life?"

"Yes."

"Ye sure?"

"Oh, yes."

"What makes ye happy, then?"

Never in my life has a man sat me down and started asking me questions like this. Uncle James only wants to talk about himself. At home, everyone whinges and moans about lack of money, neighborhood gossip, or who has aggrieved whom.

In the changing room, the guys talk about sex, or what happened on the pitch. Jody is all about making deals, using my face and body to get his percentage of my fee.

No one asks me if I'm *happy*. What does happiness have to do with work?

What a daft question.

"My family," Jason says slowly. "My house. Looking around at the life I've built and remembering each step."

"Ye've nae regrets?"

"Oh, I have plenty of those."

"Like what?"

"Hmm. Well, I wish I'd spent more time with the girls when they were little. I sometimes wish I'd made more money so life could have been easier, but it was always a tradeoff. Money versus time. It's a zero-sum game."

"Aye. Ye're right about that."

"But that's about it. I'm simple, Hamish. You strike me as simple, too."

"How did ye get so philosophical so quickly wi'out a beer in yer hand, Jason?"

His eyes catch mine.

"Easy. I realized you're courting my youngest daughter."

Amy

The landline won't stop ringing.

"Ignore it again!" Mom calls out from her throne at the kitchen table. "It's more of the biddies."

"They won't stop calling!" Carol complains. The front door opens and Shannon appears, holding a squirming, adorable preschooler on one hip and a bag of groceries on the other.

"Do they want an invitation because David Beckham's taller ginger twin is here?" Shannon asks, slightly out of breath. Her three-year-old, Ellie, makes a beeline for Mom.

"Oof!" Mom says as Ellie climbs into her lap. Declan appears behind Shannon, deposits a large box on the kitchen counter, and follows their daughter, helping to balance her so Mom's not in pain.

He plants a quick kiss on Mom's cheek as well, which makes me smile.

Having a billionaire for a brother-in-law is objectively weird. No one warns you growing up that one of your siblings might fall in love with an extraordinarily powerful and wealthy man, and that one day you'll be spending holidays with him, all using the same bathroom from your childhood, listening to him brush his teeth, watching him show up in Armani suits but end up playing touch football in the back yard with your nephews.

In the years they've been together, he's changed. Thawed a lot, and become less judgmental. Shannon's changed, too. Having all the money you could ever want hasn't spoiled her, but it's got to be nice.

And they share it, too.

In May, I'll graduate with my MBA and no debt. How many people my age can say that? And being an in-law to the famous McCormick family means having business connections I could only dream of before, when I was a part-time undergrad struggling to make all the money columns line up.

Declan and Shannon covered my tuition.

I'm grateful, and I have to prove that I was a worthy investment.

"I still don't understand why we didn't just have everything delivered here," Declan says to Shannon as she's hugging us all. I drop the spreadsheets in my hand and give her a good squeeze. By the end of the day, we won't have the arm strength to hug a marshmallow.

"Because Dad's eyes would have bugged out if he'd seen what it cost."

"Still? We *still* have to play this game?"

We all nod.

If I struggle sometimes with the whole billionaire-family-member thing, Dad's even worse.

"Dave had everything delivered to the trunk of our SUV.

This wasn't so hard. Think of it as a mini workout," she says, giving him a quick smooch and a butt pat. "Big, strong caveman carrying provisions from the car to the kitchen. Grunt, grunt."

He relaxes microscopically and gives her the same, only he bends her back into a dip. Their kiss turns hotter by the second. By the time Dad and Hamish come back in from the man cave, they've moved from "cute, hot kiss" into "I think her gum is in his mouth now" territory.

"She needs oxygen, Dec," Dad says drily. He grins and shakes his head, moving around them.

Hamish stops and stares at them, surprisingly serious. His eyes meet mine and something's changed.

I can't look away.

DING!

The doorbell jolts me, and Hamish's gaze shifts away. I go to the door and find Mary Elizabeth standing there, holding a casserole dish.

"Hi, Amy!" she says, looking behind me. It's ten o'clock in the morning, but she is perfectly coiffed, smelling like jasmine and mint. Her silver bracelets jangle as she thrusts the dish toward me. "How's Marie?"

"Uh, she's fine, but it's very early to be here."

"Oh," she titters, gently edging toward me, forcing me to take a step backward so she can come in and close the door to keep the cold outside. "I just thought I'd help out."

Declan's voice rises in the background and her ear twitches as if it were a mating call.

"Are they here already?" she asks in a breathy voice, biting her lower lip.

"Who?"

"Those gorgeous men in your family."

My mouth flattens, pulling my smile down as I think quickly.

"We're, um, keeping the dinner very small this year. Did

my mother invite you? She's still in a great deal of pain from her broken leg."

Hamish comes up behind me and bends down to pick up a small black gym bag I hadn't noticed until now.

"Oh, you know," she waves, not answering my question, eyes on Hamish. "Hi, there! I never properly thanked you for helping during the fire." She crowds me out, practically shoving me as she reaches for Hamish's hand.

The guy is an expert at dealing with flirty women, so I abandon him and put the casserole dish on the counter.

Shannon looks at it, then me, and asks, "What's that?"

"Mary Elizabeth brought it."

She recoils with a look I understand instantly. If Thanksgiving is just family and in-laws, we're already at sixteen people.

Mom, Dad, me, Shannon, Carol, Ellie, Jeffrey, Tyler, Declan, Amanda, Andrew, Charlie, Will, James, Hamish, and Pam.

"Is Terry coming?" I ask her.

She nods.

Right. Seventeen.

Now, Mom typically hosts thirty or more people, our small Cape bursting at the edges, the two bathrooms barely enough, but it works.

This year, though? We can't.

We just... can't.

"Agnes and Corrine?" I venture, realizing that how we define family is loose, and we could manage those two if they have nowhere else to go. Yes, they're pains in the butt, but they're *our* pains in the butt, so...

"No. Corrine said her daughter is doing a big holiday spread this year, so they're going to that."

DING!

Shannon and I look at each other.

"Is that a delivery?" I ask.

"No. Dec and I brought all the remaining stuff. What on Earth…"

"Hello, there," we hear Hamish's voice. "Yes, I am. Aye."

Setting her knife down, Shannon wipes her hands on her apron and starts toward the door. Hamish appears suddenly in her path, bearing three trays of cookies, big hands splayed to balance it all.

"Is this part o' the holiday? People randomly show up at yer door wi' foodstuffs?"

"No."

"Then what is it?"

"It's you."

"Me?"

"They want you to stuff their turkey."

"Why would they need *me* to put ma hand up their–oh."

"Yes, oh."

He makes a sound in the back of his throat.

DING!

Mom smiles as the doorbell rings again. Carol sees me looking at Mom, and then we both realize what's happening.

Something cunning lurks in Marie Jacoby's grin.

"Mom! Did you tell them to come? Invite them?"

"What? No!" But the smile persists. "They insisted on helping, and who am I to turn down offers of assistance from my large circle of good friends? It would hurt their feelings."

Carol's jaw sets in that determined way she's had since we were kids. "How many more are coming?"

"I don't know. A bunch of them texted me yesterday after the fire, so I posted my list."

"List? You *posted* it online?"

Shannon lifts the lid on the casserole from Mary Elizabeth. "This is scalloped potatoes and ham! It's one of the dishes we're supposed to make!"

Dad walks into the kitchen, holding a large pecan pie aloft. "Incoming!"

Mom sits at the table, the cast sticking out like it's seceding from the rest of her. Ellie is coloring quietly on the chair next to hers, eyeing the fresh white canvas of Mom's cast with increasing interest.

"How many women are here?"

Dad points to the scalloped potatoes, the cookies, and the pie. "Three."

"So far," Carol mutters.

"Where are they?"

"Trying to turn themselves into Hamish's new scandal," Shannon says with a chuckle.

As I crane my neck to watch the three women fawning over Hamish, our cat slinks around the corner. Chuckles hates everyone except Declan, so this should be interesting.

"Wait. What do you mean, new scandal?" I ask Shannon. She gives me a crooked grin and goes back to chopping onions.

"Don't you read your newsfeed? He keeps sleeping with the wrong women."

At the words *sleeping with*, something inside me shuts off and turns on at the same time.

"Wrong women?"

"He's really close to becoming a seven-figure endorsement guy in sports. You've seen his naked cover on *Sports Illustrated*, right?"

"Who hasn't? It was in every grocery store checkout lane." I won't admit that's not the only place I've seen it.

Hamish was right. I have my own copy in my bedroom closet.

"When you reach that level, image cultivation is everything."

"Of course."

"Well... "

Before Shannon can tell me the story, Hamish interrupts.

"DECLAN!" he booms from the front door. "Could ye give me a hand here? I need some assistance."

Declan is drinking a small glass of orange juice, Ellie reaching for it. Hamish has all three women fighting for his attention, and the tone of his voice is clear:

Rescue me.

Declan holds the juice glass up like a toast. "Sounds like you're doing fine all by yourself, Hamish," he calls.

"I have to go fer a run," he announces from the kitchen doorway, the gym bag clutched to his chest like a shield. "Excuse me, ladies. I need to go change."

Carol lets out a disgusted sigh through her nose. She's looking at the Excel spreadsheet that I printed out last night and taped to the refrigerator. "Mom's not kidding. Each of those women brought something from the list!"

"Good. But... does this mean we have to let them stay?"

Carol walks over to Mom and bends down, hand on her shoulder. They have a quiet but fierce conversation, Mom's eyes shrewd, Carol's voice strained.

She stands, returning to me.

"Mom says she didn't invite any of them for dinner. They're just bringing the food out of the goodness of their hearts."

"Their hearts aren't what they hope Hamish touches."

He reappears at that moment, descending the stairs from the bathroom. He's wearing a black compression shirt with red piping, black compression shorts so tight that it's clear he manscapes, grey ankle socks, black leather running shoes– and a grin of relief.

My breath disappears.

I didn't know that just looking at someone could change the shape of the world.

There's a richness to his body, a larger-than-life aura. Not just because he's a world-class athlete. If it were that simple,

I'd feel this way watching the Olympics, or that time I met Julian Edelman when I worked at a coffee shop.

No.

He has an inner confidence. A sense of being fully immersed in the world, in this moment, in the now. I want to be in his orbit, not for any specific reason, but simply because he *is*.

And because time stops when he's near.

"Well, ladies," he says with a single hand clap. "It's time fer me to go. The next few hours are ma workout."

"Where?" Their eyes light up... and the doorbell rings. Again.

"Let's make this a game," Carol says. "Mom's Thanksgiving Bingo." She checks the Excel printout. "Any guesses? Sweet potato and marshmallow bake? Yeast rolls? I'm going to make Bingo cards right now."

"Did any of them bring a duck or a chicken? We could build a tur-duck-en," I joke.

Half joke.

I wouldn't put it past these ladies to bring an actual duck and a chicken at this rate.

"Do we have any idea how many women are bringing dishes?" Shannon asks, looking at the boxes of groceries she and Declan trucked in. "Where are we going to put all this food?" she groans.

"How many dishes are on the list?" I ask Carol, who is poring over my spreadsheet and slowly checking off items.

She looks up at me, then Shannon. "I think we'll need to use the garage fridge for overflow. Worst case, I can get Jeffrey over here and he can walk some of this to my house."

"I feel really guilty not inviting them to stay," Shannon says. Hamish is starting to stretch in the hallway, laughing it up with his gaggle of admirers.

"I don't," I snap.

Shannon and Carol snicker.

"We have so much cooking to do, and setting the table, and... and suddenly, we have a house full of unexpected guests?" I point out.

DING!

It's going to be a long day.

And it's not even eleven in the morning.

6

Hamish

I'm accustomed to hordes of women descending on me.

Usually not while they're carrying casserole dishes or biscuits, but that's an added plus.

None of these women are my type, but they're nice enough, eyes shining and smiling at me with an energy I can't ignore. Have to give some of it back to them, aye?

It's how I work.

As Jason said earlier, I'm a simple man.

Emotion is a funny thing. You might think the world revolves around money, or fame, or power, and you wouldn't be wrong. But emotion is a flow of energy between people.

Not that new-agey crap, as my mum calls it. I'm talking about the dynamic when someone looks at you with lust. Or when you miss a goal and your manager tells you you're losing it.

You know it was an impossible kick to make from that angle, that he's just trying to motivate you, but then you spend the next month perfecting that kick and you hit it in the finals.

We're primed to pick up on emotion. We respond to it by instinct, then take what flows back to us, an endless circle that starts in the womb and ends with our last breath.

So, of course, I give back to these lovely women. They won't get what they think they want–my body–but I'll give them what they need.

Attention.

We all want to be seen. Loved. Appreciated.

Some of us, like James, demand to be admired.

"Declan!" I call, thumbing toward the front door. "I'm going fer a 10k, then sprints. Ye up for it?"

He freezes, eyes narrowing.

I've gone and done it.

I triggered the McCormick Competition Gene.

Da told me it was a thing in our family line, but I didn't believe it until I started mingling with my American cousins. Declan and Andrew set the bar high. They compete over everything: work, sex, babies, coffee, cars.

I suspect they compete over who can pee the longest at a urinal. Change a nappy the fastest. Drive the finest car.

Build the best empire.

I understand. *More* than understand, in fact. I'm an athlete–being competitive is how I've gotten where I am.

But needing to win is different from wanting to win. Just like needing something is different from wanting something.

Or *someone*.

Amy's eyes meet mine and she smirks.

"You two are impossible," she says, which tells me something important. The woman knows how to read a room.

That's rarer than you'd think.

"I didn't bring workout clothes," Declan says regretfully, touching his sweater. He puffs up. "Or I absolutely would work out with you."

"I'd lend you something, but I'm not exactly your size," Jason jokes.

"Remember when I had to lend you my period sweats on my first date with Declan?" Shannon says with a nostalgic smile. Her father slowly closes his eyes as if in pain.

"What's a period sweat?" I ask.

Jason now turns a shade of pink as Amy rolls her eyes.

"Tell me you know nothing about women without telling me you know nothing about women," she mutters under her breath.

"Is it like hot flashes? Because ma Mum is going through the change right now, and I know all about that. Unfortunately." Like Marie, my mother can't keep anything to herself.

"Sweat pants," Shannon says pleasantly. "For when you're bloated and uncomfortable and all you want to do is sit in front of the television, eat a pint of ice cream, and dream of Lucifer."

"Yer period makes ye want the devil?"

"Why don't you just go for your run?" Declan says, steering me toward the door. "A run I would absolutely do if I had the right clothes," he adds in a slightly louder voice as his little girl comes running over, big green eyes looking up at me.

Genetics. Moss-green eyes turn up somewhere in every generation of McCormicks. Male or female, darker hair or lighter–it's a bloodline trait, and it persists. My Da says his and James's father had them, too.

"Wanna go for a run wit' you, too," she says firmly, pointing at her wee rainbow-colored trainers. When she stomps one foot, flashing lights appear on the sides. "I can run fast!"

"Aye, lassie. Bet ye can." I bend down to look at her at eye level, as much as I can given our foot-plus height difference. "Are ye ready? It's a hard run."

"Ready!"

"Ohh," says Marie from the living room, the sound echoed by two other women. I don't remember their names, so we'll just call them Yam Bake and Cranberry Sauce.

"Let me get her coat," Declan says with a grin. "Can't wait to see Ellie beat you." As he grabs a pink wool garment, he winks at me.

See? Competitive.

DING!

I reach for the doorknob, because why not? At this point, I'm an honorary member of the Jacoby family.

A woman holding something truly useful stands before me. Her arms are laden with a case of Guinness.

"Well, hello there!" she squeaks, voice going way up. Like all the other women, she's my mother's age or older, and in perfect makeup.

Amy pushes past me, the feel of her hand on my arm setting me alight.

"Hi, Rosie. What's this?"

"Oh, Marie told me that you needed beer." She flutters her eyelashes at me. "I thought I'd help out with your Thanksgiving. You poor dears."

Amy scrunches her nose at the twelve-pack. "Guinness? Dad never buys that kind. Mom told you to get this?"

I reach over and take the burden from poor Rosie's arms. "I think what Amy means to say is thank ye." I wink at her. "And ye have nice taste in beer."

"MOM!" Amy hollers around me. With lungs that strong, it's no wonder she's a marathoner. "Did you ask Rosie to bring Guinness?"

"YES!" Marie screeches back.

"WHY?"

"FOR HAMISH!"

Amy's lips set in a line as hard as my boaby at dawn's first light, and her nostrils flare.

"Thank ye, Marie! And thank ye, Rosie."

Rosie blushes.

Amy burns.

"Aymish!" little Ellie says, splendid in her pink coat, stomping her feet to show off the flashing lights in her shoes. "Are you ready?"

"Let me put this down in the kitchen, then we go!"

I walk back to the kitchen, set the case on the floor, and return to the foyer. Ellie's dimpled hand finds mine as we step out into the snow.

Where I'm from, snow is different. We get plenty of it, but not like they have here in New England. It's late November, so there's some on the ground, but not too much. It's all compacted, a few days old.

The roads are immaculate; paved paths, though, not so much. The area in front of Marie and Jason's house is fine, but the house to the right has footprints pressed into the old snow, with a few yellow spots that make me suspect wee Chuffy's been marking some territory.

Behind me, Declan is shoving his arms into his coat to come outside with us. I bend down to Ellie.

"So ye want to race me?"

"YA!"

"Think yer faster than me?"

She looks up, eyes narrowing. Looks just like her Da. Her uncle, too.

Competitiveness is inborn, easy to spot even in a three-year-old.

"Imma cream you."

I give her Da a look. He stares at his daughter with unfiltered adoration and says, "There is no question you are my child."

A crowd of hens forms at the window, Carol off to one edge, turning her head back to speak to someone. The window slides up, and Amy bends down to shout through the screen.

"I'll bet anyone a dollar that Ellie wins!"

Ellie looks at her auntie and nods.

"Why don't ye come out here and join us?" I call to her as Declan shoves his hands in his pockets and whispers race tips in his daughter's ear.

Now, of course I'm letting Ellie win. I'm no arsehole. Might be a competitive bastard who can't stand to be bested, but even I have limits.

And a heart.

"I wouldn't want to embarrass you," Amy calls back, making people laugh.

"Ye canna embarrass me. I'm impervious to it."

"That's obvious from the women you date."

Someone mutters, "Oooh, burn."

It's Amy's father.

"Ye seem awfully fixated on who I have ma arm around on social media, Amy. Jealous?"

Before she can answer, Jason laughs. His comment earlier about courting Amy took the wind out of my sails. He was dead serious, and he strikes me as a man of honor.

Very different from my uncle James.

Jason laughed after he made the courting comment, but the point was made: He saw what he saw.

And had his say.

A tug on my shorts makes me look down. Little Ellie is so serious.

"I want to run, Aymish. Ready, set, go!"

And then she takes off down the paved walkway, shoe lights flying like fireworks.

I run behind her and the laughter follows, the audience fun to play with. Amy's still in the window, watching. Excellent peripheral vision is a must for a footballer, and it comes in handy in situations like this, too.

Two long lunges and I gain on Ellie, pulling into the lead just enough to see how truly McCormick she is. Motivated to win, she speeds up. I slow down to give her the edge as we cross the finish line.

I sweep her up to my shoulders just before she hits an ice patch, and she screams, "I won!" Giggles cover my head, her tiny fingers finding purchase in my hair.

"Again! Again!"

"He's a natural with kids," I hear Shannon say to Declan as she joins him outside, his arm wrapping around her shoulders.

"I should be," I shout back. "Have enough wee brothers and sisters."

"When do you plan to have one of your own?" Jason calls out.

"Imagine the gingers Hamy and Amy could make!" Marie shrieks.

Amy disappears behind the curtain.

Shannon disengages herself from Declan and his arms reach up to my head, his little girl handed off. I'm taller by an inch or two and I can tell it bothers him. The man isn't accustomed to looking up at anyone.

"Last chance, Amy!" I call toward the window as I begin to stretch, ready to do my training. I give Ellie a fist bump. "You won," I whisper to her with a wink. "But don't tell anyone. I canna have people thinking I'm no' a good runner."

"I won!" she shrieks. "ME! I beat Aymish!"

Aye.

She's such a McCormick.

Amy

The counter and fridge are full, and the table out on the deck, too.

Mom's sneaky plan has worked.

"Scalloped potatoes and ham?"

I locate the dish. "Yes."

Carol is reading from a list app on her phone, one I forced her and Shannon to download. She taps the screen.

"Green bean casserole?"

"Yes."

"Cranberry sauce?"

"Yes, but homemade." I sniff the gelatinous concoction, trying not to retch. I hate cranberry sauce, all kinds. "I think it has orange and clove in it."

"Hmm. Good thing we have canned. Cookie tray?"

"Candy cane cookies, peanut butter buckeyes, pfefferneuse, thumbprint cookies with Maine blueberry jam, and lace cookies."

"Wow. All those kinds? I can't believe so many people brought cookies."

"Oh, no–those are just from Janice." I point to the array of green, red, and white plastic platters, wrapped in clear wrap. "Five different batches."

Carol pats her belly. "I'm going to just get fatter and fatter until you can't tell the difference between my breasts and my stomach." She eyes my midsection. "Why aren't you chubby like me and Mom?"

"Because I run?"

"You've lost a ton of weight in the last few years. Running? Really?"

I shrug. "I like it. Burns off my anxiety."

"And your second set of breasts."

"Did I make the wrong choice?" I mutter as I catalog the fridge's contents.

"Wrong choice about what?"

"Should I have gone for a run with Hamish?"

"Is 'gone for a run' a euphemism for sleeping with him? If so, yes. You made the wrong choice to say no."

"Stop! I'm not sleeping with him! I just think a run would do me good. Stress relief."

"Orgasms are better stress relief. Orgasms with a hot international athlete."

"You have a one-track mind."

"You say that as if it's a bad thing."

"I don't tease you about Terry."

She reels back. "Terry?"

"Yeah. Terry."

"What about him?"

"It's obvious you like him. I don't tease you about that, so quit teasing me about Hamish."

"What?" Her high giggle sounds like Mom. "Of course I don't have a thing for Terry."

"Mmm hmmm."

"He's totally not my type!"

"Right. Not an ex-con, has money, no tattoos, and no personality disorder."

"Hey! That's not... That was just Todd. That's not my type."

I offer her a lace cookie. She smartly shoves it in her mouth, because she knows I'm right.

"You're wrong," she mumbles around the mouthful of yum. "And I can't go after Terry McCormick. Are you kidding me? It's bad enough Amanda married Declan's brother. We can't have our entire family tree turn into a Mobius strip. My kids and Shannon's kids would be double cousins."

"I don't think that's a thing. And Jeffrey and Tyler wouldn't be his."

Something hits the back of my knee, making it buckle slightly, a sharp pain on my tendon making me yelp.

"Are you talking about someone you're secretly dating, Carol?" The object that hit me was the edge of the footrest on Mom's wheelchair. She's slowly getting used to wheeling herself around, but her steering is about on the level of an overcaffeinated eight-year-old on a bumper car ride.

Shannon walks behind her, Ellie perched on one hip, sucking on an applesauce pouch like a baby Dyson.

"What's left for us to make?" She watches Carol repositioning the big tent of foil over the roaster.

"Right," Carol says, turning to pick up her phone from the table. "Stuffing?"

"In the bird, and a casserole dish of extra."

"Mashed potatoes?"

"Celine from my yoni yoga class brought some, with cream cheese and chives mashed in. Yum!" Mom crows.

"I can't believe you conned all those women into cooking Thanksgiving dinner for us," Shannon says, shaking her head.

"I can," Carol replies. "Bet Mom gave them copies of her recipe cards, even."

Our mother has suddenly lost the ability to make eye contact.

"Why?" I venture. "Why would you do that?"

"They asked how they could help after they learned my vigorous, vibrant sex life ruined Thanksgiving!"

"This conversation is what's ruining it, Mom," I inform her.

Behind me, Carol screams.

"MOM! Chuffy's trying to hump the turkey!"

The little bichon has managed to jump up on the counter and he's trying to paw the aluminum foil off the pan.

"Ewww! Gross! Get down, Chuffy! You'll get salmonella," Mom scolds as Carol grabs the dog, whose toenails have pierced the foil. It's hanging from his paw like a surreal kite.

"*That's* what you're worried about? That the *dog* will get sick? Now what? We need a new turkey," Shannon says as she inspects the bird.

"Of course we don't. We'll just do what we did the last time," Mom says casually.

"The *last* time?" I start to retch.

"As long as you cook it, all the bacteria goes away. And besides, dog's mouths are sterile."

"No, they're not! Who told you that?"

"I read it on the internet."

"Did he actually touch the turkey?" Shannon asks, eyeing it.

I point to the one spot up by the neck where I saw his paw land. "Other than that spot? No."

"*Whew.*" Shannon grabs a knife off the butcher block and slices the piece off, throwing it in the trash. "Because if he had, I was about to make a bad decision."

"If you did, I wouldn't blame you. Look at who spawned us. Plus, we're how many hours into this holiday marathon we didn't plan on?"

"Too many. I'm starting to feel like a reality-show contestant."

"Mom has a way of doing that to people."

"To be fair," I whisper, hating to admit it, "she's really taking our request seriously."

"I know, right? Staying out of our hair."

"Did Dad slip her an edible or something? Because she's so calm. Not interfering at all."

"What's the trouble?" Hamish asks, walking through the back door. He's dripping with sweat. His compression shirt, already tight and now wet, reveals the topography of every hair, every vein, every pore on his body.

"Nothing," I snap.

"The dog tried to eat the turkey," Carol explains.

Hamish looks down at his feet, where Chuckles is rubbing against his ankle. Chuffy is sitting on his haunches, panting happily, eyes on his own personal ginger god, who might throw him a table scrap.

Hamish laughs. "It's as if the cat and the wee dog joined forces to get possession of the bird."

"Cats and dogs don't form strategic alliances like that, Hamish."

"I'm telling ye, those animals are plotting against you. Especially the blastie."

"Blastie?"

"The grumpy cat."

"That's paranoid."

"I've nae reason no' to be."

"I thought you were out for a long run."

"That was just part one. Came back for hydration. Sprints are next."

"How many hours a day do you work out, Hamish?" Carol asks, interested, as Shannon unrolls fresh foil and recovers the turkey. Chuckles eyes her like a diamond thief determining the exact position of laser alarms in a gem store.

"However many I need to stay in peak shape." He tips his head back and practically pours an entire twenty-ounce bottle of electrolyte drink down his throat, the long, thick lines of his neck fascinating to watch as he swallows. Hamish McCormick is radiating heat and sweat from his run. I can't avoid his scent, can't stop feeling his warmth, can't not hear the little guttural sounds of his swallowing and his breath.

DING!

Carol's on her phone negotiating with my older nephew, Jeffrey. Something about making his little brother take a bath before coming over. Shannon's nowhere to be seen, and Hamish doesn't live here, so I guess I'm the one answering the doorbell.

What's left to make? Maybe the parade of women coming to ogle Hamish will start bringing wine.

Declan's executive assistant, Dave, is standing at the door, holding a garment bag folded over his arm.

"Is Hamish here?" he asks.

"Oh, my God. Men, too?"

"Excuse me?"

"What did my mother tell you to bring?" I sniff the air and look around for a box or bag. "I smell yeast. Let me guess. Hot buns?"

"This is Hamish McCormick's suit." I get an epic eye roll before he turns around and walks back to a small compact car parked on the street, hazard lights flashing.

Why would Hamish need a suit?

I go back into the kitchen and thrust the garment bag at him.

"Here."

"What's this?"

"Your suit."

"Ma suit? How did this get here?"

"Declan's assistant just delivered it."

Bzzz

Hamish's hip comes alive. Given how skin tight his compression shorts are, I'm wondering where he hides his phone, but sure enough, he pulls it out and looks at his texts.

"James says he had ma suit couriered over. Says he wants some candid shots of us here at dinner."

"Us?" Dad asks, everyone within earshot suddenly giving Hamish their full attention. What is James up to now?

"Him and me. No' the whole family. Says the house is a bit downscale, but it'll fit in wi' something where he helps the puir."

The tips of Dad's ears turn red.

Uh oh.

He's mad. Dad doesn't get mad very often.

"James said *what*?" he asks Hamish.

Who sighs, deeply.

"I dinna understand him either."

Declan snorts. "Join the club."

It dawns on me that I have no idea why Hamish is in Boston, yet again.

"Why are you here, Hamish?"

"Amy!" Dad scolds me. "That's rude. We invited him!"

"I don't mean it that way. I mean, why are you in Boston at all?"

"I'm here to do a commercial with James."

That makes Declan freeze. "Commercial?"

"Aye. His new campaign."

"Campaign? He's running for *office?*" Pure horror covers my brother-in-law's face. It should. The idea of James McCormick being an elected official makes me want to weep for the entire state.

"No," Hamish says with a laugh. "An ad campaign."

"For what?" Declan's relief is palpable.

"Anterdec."

"But what, specifically?"

Hamish reels back a bit. "Ye know, I didna ask. Something about being the world's wisest man. Suave, too."

Everyone groans.

"You didn't bother to find out what you're endorsing?" I jump in, genuinely astonished, but also not truly surprised.

He shrugs. "He's family. I'm stuck here in the States. And he's paying me."

I scoff. "You're so..."

He winks. "I think the word yer searching fer is *irresistible*."

"Simple."

He just lays the suit over a chair and jogs into the back yard, where he begins sprinting, as if *that's* how you wrap up a conversation.

He thinks he can dismiss me like that? He thinks he can win?

"Not enough popcorn in the world for this," Carol murmurs. Shannon laughs.

Dad turns to her and Declan. "Do you really think James is coming here with a *photographer?*"

Declan pulls out his phone. "Let me get Dave on it. I'll make sure Dad doesn't turn Thanksgiving into a media circus."

"That's not a no. Jesus. What is James thinking? And that 'poor' comment..."

For a moment, all I can do is watch Hamish, who wasn't kidding. He's doing sprints in the fenced-in yard, running as fast as possible from one end to the other.

Chuffy runs head first into the glass slider, tail wagging so fast, I half expect him to take flight like a tiny helicopter. As he barks, Chuckles hisses and slinks off.

"Dad is thinking about himself," Declan says, head bent down over his phone, "as usual."

"You know anything about this campaign Hamish is talking about?" Dad asks Declan as I move away, otherwise distracted by two hundred pounds of pure fascination.

Reluctant fascination.

My attention wanders to the back yard. I watch Hamish doing sprint after sprint, over and over, each one as enthusiastically brutal as the last. His legs are a work of art. I'll give him that.

Soccer player legs are a thing. Tree trunks in muscled form, they're huge and powerful, developed by years of daily footwork and bold runs. He's a cocky jerk, but a premier player like Hamish doesn't get to his level without a crushing amount of hard body work.

He just keeps going, sprint after sprint, ignoring the dripping sweat, until he stops to drink, then...

Starts again.

My boots are by the front door, so I pass Dad and Declan, who are laughing together about James being a sophisticated older man. Massachusetts winters mean the heavy boots come out in late October. I'm fine without a coat today, my sweats warm enough, but no way will I head out there bootless.

The yard gets plenty of sun, so the ground he's running on is tan, dead grass, but there's a perimeter of snow at the base of the fence, where it's always in the shade. It's cold enough for the top layer of dirt to be frozen, but the terrain is uneven.

Nothing like a soccer field.

"It's not flat like the fields you're used to playing on," I call out from a small spot of clear concrete on the patio.

"Pitch."

"Excuse me? Did you just call me a *bitch?*"

That makes him stop, brow down, sweat dripping from copper-colored ringlets, true horror in his eyes. "What? Nae! I said pitch. With a P."

"What's a pitch?"

"A field. A *soccer* field." He says soccer the way I say, well... His name.

Dripping with sarcasm.

"Are you capable of having a single conversation with me that doesn't involve insults or sex?"

"I was about to ask ye the same, Amy."

He starts doing burpees, flat on the ground, balancing on palms and toes, then pulling his feet up to his hips and springing upright with arms in the air.

The flow of his coordinated movement is so seamless. By the time I can think of a reply, he's done five in a row.

"How do you do that?"

"Do what?"

"That." I wave in his general direction.

"Burpees?"

"All of it. You're so athletic."

He laughs. "It's ma job."

"It's more than a job to you."

"Aye. Ye noticed."

"You work really hard. I mean, I run, but you take it up a notch."

"Have to. I'm aging out. If I dinna stay in shape, I'll be cut from the team. Need a few more good years to maximize the endorsement contracts."

"What's the average length of a career for a Scottish football player?"

A smile stretches his face even as he continues the burpees. "Ye wanna know ma length?"

"Good God, Hamish! You're proving me right at every turn," I reply, but I can't help but laugh.

Damn it.

"That's a good question wi' nae easy answer–"

The sound of the sliding glass door opening makes us both turn to find little Ellie on the deck, shoes on, grinning, clearly cooking something up in that little preschool brain.

"Wanna race, Aymish?"

Before either of us can say a word, Chuffy sprints outside, a shriek coming behind him.

Because he has Dad's smoked turkey.

Except the dog's entire head is inside the turkey's body.

Sprinting faster than any soccer player going for a long goal, his white, fluffy butt and tiny tail moving faster than a dremel at high speed is a sight that takes my brain a few extra seconds to comprehend.

Because eighty percent of Chuffy is now a roasted, gleaming turkey with a bichon bum.

He's a tur-dog-en.

Huh. I guess we got a version of that tur-duck-en I joked about earlier.

Be careful what you joke about, right? Thanksgiving is serving up some truly bizarre karma this year.

Blind and overexcited, the dog heads straight for Hamish, who sidesteps him quickly, his face reflecting my astonishment. My stomach drops as I realize the turkey's a goner. All of Dad's hard work smoking it is–

Oh, no.

A second turkey appears at ground level. This one is moving in starts and stops as Chuckles drags it across the dead grass by one hind leg.

We make eye contact.

The cat's look says, *I have finally bested you, stupid human. Behold my conquest.*

Dad runs into the back yard, agog as he looks back and forth, Chuffy now ramming his turkey-body head over and over into the wooden fence.

Ellie starts clapping and chasing Chuffy, who backs up as she gets closer and runs like a drunken sailor with a fire-cracker up his ass.

"I left the turkeys on the counter for one damn minute!" Carol screams as she runs out, just socks on her feet. She lunges after Chuckles' turkey by instinct, the air around the turkey's body warm and misty.

I stop her with my hand on her forearm. "It's pointless."

"Aye," Hamish says, stepping around us, leaning against the fence. His eyes meet mine with so much mirth, I can't help but return the smile.

Again.

Then he looks at Chuffy and Chuckles with their respective bounties and says with an arched eyebrow and a grin:

"I'm no' being paranoid if I'm *right*."

Hamish

"Too bad we can't just shoot one of the turkeys in that flock that's been wandering around the edges of the neighborhood," Marie calls out from her throne, angled between the kitchen and the living room. Someone's left the sliding glass door open, everyone a bit dazed by the spectacle.

"Aye. Saw some on the trail when I was running," I call back to her. Amy and Jason are wrangling the dog and cat, pulling the half-eaten turkey carcasses away, Jason careful not to let the meat touch the dead grass, then giving up.

Chuckles begins gagging.

"Hairball?" I ask Amy, who winces and turns away from the cat.

"Wishbone, I think," Jason says, lifting the kitty out of our sight.

"I still dinna understand this holiday. Ye cook two birds

and let the animals steal them both? Why would ye let yer pets win?"

"Close the door!" Carol snaps. "We don't live in a barn!"

Amy obediently goes inside. I follow, all of us now in the kitchen as Jason handles the pets and mourns the twin turkey deaths.

Second death, I supposed. They were already quite deceased when the roasting began.

"We haven't even *had* the holiday yet!" Marie whimpers. "And the cat and dog normally don't do this."

"'Normally'," Carol echoes, using finger quotes. "You just told us Chuffy's humped the turkey before."

"Humped it. Not *eaten* it!"

"Do you not see that those are equally gross, Mom? Because that would be disturbing. Every childhood dinner now has to be cast through a new memory lens," Carol says with a shudder.

"You know what's a disturbing cast, Carol? This!" She points to her leg. "Breaking my leg and then watching my beloved holiday fall apart because you couldn't bother to monitor the pets! I can't believe you let them eat *both* turkeys!"

"ME? You're blaming *me*? It's not my fault you and Dad go at it like horny teenagers on a conjugal visit. A sex swing, Mom? Really?"

"Don't you dare judge my sex life, Carol. At least I have one!"

Declan clears his throat, leaning in to me. "Welcome to the Jacoby family."

Carol screeches and Marie shoots it right back, the two blasting each other.

I laugh softly at Declan's comment. "This? Eh. Makes me feel right at home."

"Your parents are like Jason and Marie?"

"Ye mean the sex swing nonsense? God, na. We dinna

routinely talk about ma Da's todger in public. I meant the whinging and the moaning."

Jason contemplates his wife and eldest daughter, who are now engaged in an insult competition. It's clear he's considering stepping in to referee.

If football has taught me nothing else, it's that the referee has the worst job on the planet. Everyone hates him. He can never please everyone, and when the game's over, no one remembers him unless they hold a grudge. Which they often do.

A smart man would walk away, and Jason does, tapping me on the shoulder.

"You a steak man?"

"Aye. I'm all about protein."

"We've got some in the garage freezer. I could use a hand bringing them in."

"Ye seem verra calm about the pets eating yer dinner."

"It happened. I adjust fast. Can't waste energy getting upset about how things could have gone differently. You have to do what makes sense next."

"Ye'd make a fine footballer with that approach."

He pats his belly. "A little old for that."

"I'd hazard a guess ye've played soccer." The word feels like paste in my mouth, but I say it.

"Actually, I coach Jeffrey and Tyler's teams."

I look around. "Where are the lads?"

"Biking over. We had them stay home until one o'clock."

"One? It's one? I'm behind on ma training."

Declan, meanwhile, is watching me with the cool, calculating eyes of a man who has something at stake.

Out of the corner of my eye, I see Amy bent down, petting Chuffy's belly. The dog's head is a greasy mess, his white fur turned a sickly gray. Her mouth curves in a relaxed smile as she tilts her head, loving on the dog.

It's as relaxed as I've ever seen her, and I can't help but smile. She's a mystery.

Families like this produce good people. Nice, kind people who go through life seeking others like them. If Jason coaches football, he's someone who sees potential in children. You can't be that kind of person and not be fundamentally decent.

Well, you can. There are asshole coaches out there. But Jason isn't one of them.

"I see you watching her," Jason says casually. He and Declan track their eyes over to Amy, who is closing the sliding glass door, leaving the dog outdoors.

"I'm no' really courting her, Jason."

Declan does a double take. "Courting?"

I laugh. "Jason accused me of courting Amy earlier."

"That's a very old-fashioned term," Declan says, more serious than I expect. "Are you?"

"Of course no'."

His jaw tightens. "You're not really planning to sleep with her, are you?"

Saying such a thing in front of a woman's father is poor decorum at best, and grounds for a beating back home. I'm an affable guy, and I try to keep life nice and light. But sometimes, I just can't do it.

This is one of those times.

"Yer own love life so bleak, ye have to ask about mine, Declan?"

I've hit a nerve. Can actually see it twitch in his neck, right along the carotid artery.

Jason's shoulders expand with a long, deep inhale, but he stays quiet. We've followed him outside and we're now steps away from a faded white side door to the garage, metal from the looks of it. The lower half is scarred with a series of dents.

"Not talking about my wife with you. I'm making sure

Amy's safe," Declan says, hands in his pockets. His voice is so calm that if he ever changed careers and became a hitman, he'd be undetectable.

"Safe? From me? Ye think I'm a threat?"

"I think you like to play, Hamish. Amy isn't a toy."

Ah. A light switch flips in me.

"Only thing I play with is a ball on a pitch."

"You pitch your balls to a lot of women. Newsfeed makes that clear."

"What I do in ma spare time is none of yer business, Cousin."

"It is when it involves Amy."

"She's a grown woman wi' her own free will." A hard feeling comes over my skin, a force field engaged. The changing room is where I usually feel this. The jabs and jeers from my teammates after a mistake on my part sometimes go a bit too far, requiring a show of strength to make them back down.

Never thought I'd face it like this, with family. Guess there's always something new to learn about people.

Declan nods, his silence deadlier than any reply. He doesn't blink, just watches me.

"All of my daughters are," Jason says, with the hush of a man controlling his emotions. "They're smart and capable and strong, but they're just as vulnerable as anyone else. Amy's our baby. I feel protective of her. Maybe because she's the last one I can be protective of. Shannon has Declan. Carol's about as hardened as a woman can be, after what her ex put her through."

Declan is staring me down like a Beefeater with a crowd of schoolboys trying to make him react.

Jason opens the garage door. I follow him in, Declan at my heels.

The garage is packed, neatly, with yard-grooming

supplies, an old, wheezing fridge, and a big white freezer that looks like you could store a body in it.

I cut Declan a side glance and wonder if that thought's occurred to him, too.

Jason opens the freezer and starts handing me plastic-wrapped frozen steaks.

"Todd was charming. Smooth. Knew how to work a room. Didn't have the success you have, Hamish, but he had something similar. Like he was trying to woo everyone he met. Women. Men. Dogs. Chuckles hated his guts, but he was just a little kitten when Todd went off to prison."

This is news to me.

The pile's growing bigger in my hands, the cold meat chilling my fingers.

"Carol's ex-husband went to prison?"

"Still there," Declan says, breaking his silence. Jason hands him a stack of four steaks, then adds two packages of ground beef to the top.

"Yer no' comparing me to a convict?"

"No," Jason says simply, instantly reminding me of my Da. "I'm saying that Todd played with Carol. Viewed her as a mark, not a woman with feelings. I didn't see it then, but I do now. He sorted the world into groups. Those he could charm easily. Those who took a little work. Those he could dominate and use. Those who weren't worth it."

A strange tension fills Declan's body, one of his eyebrows twitching slightly. He opens his mouth, then closes it, letting out a light breath through his nose.

"Then he'd work the room. Or the marks. Whatever word you use, Todd didn't view people as people. He viewed them as objects you arrange to get a desired outcome. *His* desired outcome. Always his."

Jason holds six steaks in one hand, balanced precariously. He shuts the freezer door and we head back to the house. I can't feel my hands any longer, but I'll call it a poor man's cryotherapy.

"That's either genius or narcissism. He's brilliant or a colossal dick," I tell Jason's back as we head to the glass slider.

"Or both," Declan adds from behind me.

"Well, I'm nae dick."

"Then prove it. Don't hurt Amy," Jason says, pausing at the door. Inside, the women are bustling in the kitchen, Carol sitting at the table with her lists and a pen, Shannon pulling her hair up with a twistie, Amy smiling wide as she listens to something Carol's saying.

At the sight of her, something in me loosens. I go warm, wanting to be in there with her.

And not just to escape the wrath of her father and brother-in-law.

"Why're ye getting so serious about this? I've never asked her out. Never gone on a date. Never..." I make a sex gesture. "We've no' so much as kissed. I just flirt. Nothing more."

"I see the gossip sites," Declan says.

"If ye judge me solely by those, I'm a walking hormone."

Declan clears his throat. "I believe your latest nickname is the Ginger Jackhammer."

"Footballers get stupid nicknames all the time."

"They weren't referring to your feet."

Both men just stare at me.

BANG BANG BANG!

We all jolt, the top steak in Jason's hands sliding off the pile and hitting the ground. Inside, a teenager with braces is waving and grinning at us through the glass door.

"Little Jeffrey isna so little, is he?" I comment. The slider opens and he joins us. Gangly, with the gawky, loose joints of a growing lad, he's a metal-mouth kid with spots all over his face.

"I heard Chuckles and Chuffy ate the turkeys," he says as

Jason hands off his steaks to the kid. "I think they were staging a protest."

"Protest?" I ask. Declan rolls his eyes and walks away. Something about that makes me think there's quite a story coming.

"Protesting Thanksgiving."

"Why would anyone protest it? It's a day to worship turkeys, nae? Seems like the dog and the cat did that just right."

Jeffrey's eyes narrow. "You're Scottish."

"Aye."

"Do you know the history of Thanksgiving?"

"No' really. Just that ye kill an innocent bird in the name o' commemorating taking o'er a new land inhabited by people who helped ye, eat until ye regret yer own gluttony, then watch a bunch o' men run around a pitch and play football wi' their hands."

"That's not what Thanksgiving is about!" Jeffrey shrieks. "Though you're right about the whole stealing land part."

"Jeffrey," Jason says, waving him and me inside. "If you're going to torture Hamish with your version, why not do it inside? I need to defrost the steaks."

"*MY version?*" Jeffrey screeches. "I'm giving him the *right* answer."

"Fine, Mr. Right," Jason says with a fatherly hand on the teen's shoulder. "Just do it inside."

Amy

Dad and Declan looked like they were ganging up on Hamish. While they were outside, looking serious, Carol, Shannon, and I planned out the rest of the day. Our biggest problem is going to be making sure we have oven space to warm all the different dishes before we eat.

Not cook–*warm*. Warm food should be served warm. Cold food should be served cold. There's nothing worse than taking a bite of stuffing that's gotten cold, or eating cranberry sauce that's warm. Everything has its optimal state, and finding that balance is crucial.

Which is why Hamish McCormick needs to leave.

Now.

I know, I know. No chance of that. But I can dream.

"So let me get this straight," I hear Hamish saying as he, Jeffrey, Dad, and Declan all come in carrying armloads of frozen steaks. "The English stormed the beaches of New England, raided the Native American villages, and forced the locals to kill turkeys and serve them to their invaders?"

"Oh, it's *way* worse than that," Jeffrey replies, taking a deep breath to prepare to unleash his next words.

"I believe it," Hamish says, crossing his arms over his broad chest. "English bastards."

"Then they killed the Native Americans, stole their land, and–"

"Thanksgiving's about being thankful!" Mom pipes up. All the nice women who dropped by to 'help' are gone–that's something to be thankful for. Mom's sipping a soda and smiling at Jeffrey. "We get together and cook a delicious meal, and we're so grateful to the nice Indians who fed the poor, starving settlers in Plymouth."

"Grandma!" Jeffrey snaps at her. "It's Native Americans. And the English settlers–"

"English *bastards*," Hamish mutters.

Declan's phone buzzes. He looks down and flinches slightly, then smiles wide a moment later. My brother-in-law is emotionally reserved, so a smile like that means one of three things. Either:

1. He made a bunch of money,

2. Sex, or...

"Dad's sick! Says he can't come today," Declan announces to the crowd.

Every single person present relaxes visibly.

"The English *bastards*," Jeffrey continues loudly, mimicking Hamish's last words with glee, "stormed the beaches, stole the land, ravished the women, and–"

"RAVISHED?" Carol shouts from the other room. "Jeffrey, where did you hear *that* word?"

"I read it on the back of some of Grandma's Harlequin romance novels. The ones in paper bags in the attic."

Dad sighs.

"It's not that you're wrong, Jeffrey. You're not. It's just that your interpretation of Thanksgiving is–"

"It's not an interpretation! It's FACTS."

"Your facts are a bit one-sided."

"So is slaughtering people in the New World and colonizing an inhabited land and destroying natural resources, which is what the English did, Grandpa."

Hamish's eyes light up. "We need to get ye to Scotland, Jeffrey. Ye'll be welcomed there wi' open arms."

Jeffrey mutters something about exploitation, old people, and going to college in Scotland as he heads toward one of the trays of cookies and disappears with a fistful of baked goods.

Declan clears his throat, dark eyebrows up. "Did everyone hear what I said? Dad can't make it."

"Hmm. Maybe my conversation with him had an impact," Dad murmurs.

Hamish and Declan both blink exactly once and turn to Dad. I see the resemblance in them, the McCormick command evident.

"Conversation?" Declan inquires.

"Called him. Told him this wasn't an event for public consumption. No cameras. Suddenly he's 'sick.'"

Dad smirks.

Bzzz

Shannon's phone buzzes now. As she looks at it, Ellie imitates her older cousin, sneaking a cookie from one of the overflowing trays on the counter. I don't say anything. I'm not the one who'll have to deal with a sugared-up kid tonight.

"Aw. Pam isn't coming. She's sick, too," Shannon announces.

"They're both sick? Same issue?"

Huddling heads, Shannon and Declan compare texts.

"Pam says she's reacting to a new medicine they're giving her for the Lyme disease."

"Dad probably has a bad case of the supermodel flu."

Hamish catches Declan's eye and they both shake their heads knowingly.

"Is it contagious? Wouldna mind catching a case o' that maself," Hamish says, my stomach dropping and jaw clenching.

Before I can answer, the front door opens and a tornado blows in.

A toddler tornado.

Amanda and Andrew's twins, Will and Charlie, are just over two, but they're like an entire baseball team of trouble. Adorable and increasingly verbal, they are also *very* active. Ellie's a busy three-year-old, but she's in slow motion compared to the boys.

Suddenly, Chuffy's yelping, Chuckles disappears up the stairs, and Mom exclaims, "Oh, my!" as Charlie climbs into her lap and starts trying to roll one wheel of her chair.

Will grabs Chuffy by the hind legs and yells, "Doggy soft! Doggy soft!" while the poor animal gives me side eye that says he'd rather be trapped in a dirty litter box with Chuckles for a week than be carried around by a toddler.

Me, too, doggy. Me, too.

Amanda extracts the little white puffball from her son's

chubby hands while Andrew lifts Charlie off Mom, planting a kiss on her cheek and pivoting gracefully to take Will from Amanda. The way they coordinate their movements is a piece of performance art. Balancing both kids on his hips, one arm wrapped around each twin as he tickles them, Andrew's athleticism shows.

Speaking of athletes, Hamish bends to give a flustered Amanda a hug and a kiss.

Her hair is the same color as his, and mine. Back in the days before our lives revolved around billionaires, she used to dye her hair for mystery shops, and the spectrum of colors was wide. Since marrying Andrew, she's stuck to more muted shades; the auburn hasn't been in rotation for a while.

For the longest time, she and Shannon–and then Carol– pushed me to work with them, but I'm glad I found my own path. Mystery shopping isn't my thing. I don't have the patience to pretend to be something I'm not, and I definitely don't suffer fools gladly.

Exhibit A: Hamish McCormick.

"Hey!" I'm in Amanda's hug before I can react, her rumbling laughter making me join in. I've never known a time when she wasn't around, my big sister's bestie like a third sister. Amanda's an only child and probably spent more time at our house than her own when we were kids.

I was never allowed into the inner sanctum of their friendship, but now that we're adults, it's starting to feel more equal.

"Hey back. How's it going in Chaosland?"

She looks at the twins, who are currently climbing Andrew like he's an activity at a New England fall fair. "Good. We're tackling potty training."

"Already?"

"They're twenty-seven months old."

"How's it going?"

"Notice they're still wearing diapers? That's how it's going."

"I'm noticing you need a drink."

Hamish slips up the stairs, not that I'm tracking him. Amanda notices me noticing him, and gives me one of those looks that says I'm never going to hear the end of whatever she's seeing.

"You two flirting?"

"If by flirting, you mean, am I plotting how to give him food poisoning, then yes."

"I heard that!" he calls down. "Canna be any worse than what the dog did to the turkey."

Questioning eyes meet mine. "Dog? Turkey?" she asks.

"Chuckles and Chuffy managed to eat both turkeys."

"WHAT?"

"It's steaks for Thanksgiving," Dad says as he gives Amanda a hug. "Thawing a small mountain of beef now."

"Excuse me?" It's Hamish, from upstairs. "Where d'ye keep yer towels? I'm taking a shower and canna find them."

"Speaking of a mountain of beef," Amanda murmurs as I swat her on my way to the bathroom.

"In the closet," I tell him from the doorway. He opens it and gives me a quizzical look. The din of people downstairs fades as I step closer to him, peering in.

No neat stack like Mom usually has.

Right. Her leg is broken.

His hand brushes my arm as he closes the door, and suddenly, he's all I know. His scent, the curve of his thick calf as I look down, the way the light through the window shines on his black workout shirt. The craziness of Thanksgiving dissolves. I've stood in this bathroom thousands of times and never felt so aware of every pore on my body.

A body that can't help but respond to him.

"I'll get some clean ones. There's a load in the dryer," I say faintly, turning on my heel and thinking about my own need for a shower. Jogging down the stairs, I bypass the crowd and stop at the washing machine, grabbing the edges for support.

"Stop it, Amy. Stop it, stop it, stop it," I tell myself. My body responds to him because biology primes it to, not because he has any redeeming qualities. Sure, I could sleep with him. He's made it clear that's what he wants.

But no way will I give him the satisfaction, even if *my* satisfaction would be guaranteed.

Angry at everything, I grab an armload of towels, throw them in an empty basket, and fold one neatly to give him. Sure, I should do the whole load, but he's waiting, and if I appear with a stack, I'll have to enter the bathroom to put them away.

I'm not sure I can manage to stand that close to him again and not lunge.

"What is wrong with me?" I mutter as I reach the bathroom and knock.

No answer.

I knock again.

No answer.

Huh. The shower's not on, so he's obviously not in there. I can just drop the towel off and go back to the kitchen. Suppressing my hormones is so much easier when I'm surrounded by my family.

The doorknob turns easily, unlocked, further confirmation that he's not...

"OH, MY GOD!" I screech at the sight of a very tall, *very* naked Hamish standing in front of the sink, brushing his teeth.

"Mufph?" he says through a mouthful of foam, eyes wide. Making no effort to cover himself, he actually turns toward me, pulling the toothbrush out of his mouth and spitting into the sink.

"WHAT ARE YOU DOING?" I ask, flinging the folded towel at him. He catches it with his free hand, the movement of his muscles irresistible as he tries to stop it from dropping to the floor. He fails, the towel now useless.

I cannot *not* watch.

It's not my fault.

"Brushing ma teeth."

"NAKED?"

"I was about to take a shower."

"Who brushes their teeth *before* taking a shower?"

"Me."

I gape at him.

A slow grin forms on his mouth, the kind he uses to flirt. The guy has zero hangups about his body, clearly.

And it's a body I'm openly watching now. I can't help it. He's five feet away from me, with skin so alive, it glows. I'm no more responsible for my reactions than I am when I sneeze.

Or orgasm.

"Like what ye see?"

"I–I'm so sorry! Wait. No. No, I'm not. Because I knocked. TWICE!"

"Ma mouth was full."

"You could have locked the door."

"Didna expect ye to barge in and ogle me."

"OGLE? I am not *ogling*."

"Yer apparently in na rush to leave."

"This isn't a locker room! Who stands in a bathroom naked?"

"Ye shower with yer clothes on? Explains a lot."

"What does that mean?"

"It means ye've a stick so far up yer arse, ye look like The Queen herself."

"If you're going to insult me, at least have the decency to cover up!"

He grabs the biggest thing on the counter and holds it over his crotch.

It's my makeup mirror.

"That's mine!" I screech, pointing.

"Ma todger's nae one else's but mine. Rather fond of it." He winks. "Happy to lend it to ye whenever ye want, though."

A thump behind me, then a gasp, tells me we're no longer alone.

8

Hamish

There's a small herd of Jacoby women staring at my nude body.

None of this is new. Women do it all the time. A few men, too.

Could I grab a towel? Of course. But watching Amy squirm is too good.

Add her sister Carol, though, and suddenly that towel is necessary. Anyone but Amy is a splash of cold water on a very hot rod.

Reading my mind, Amy tosses the dropped one at me again. I catch it one handed and wrap it around my hips. She relaxes, arms going loose, as if covering myself protects her.

Protects her from what? Me?

Or herself?

"Whoa," Carol says softly, biting her lower lip.

"HEY!" Amy shouts, shoving her older sister from the doorway and slamming the door shut. I'm left alone in the bathroom, the towel hanging, my mouth filled with peppermint and the taste of missed opportunity.

Only one thing to do now: laugh.

The sound of Amy yelling at her sister is drowned out by the shower's flow, my two-minute shower skills impeded slightly by a piece of wood in the middle of my body.

"Nae," I tell it. "No' now. Poor timing."

It'll listen. It trusts me. I give it what it needs—more than what it needs, in fact.

Perhaps a little *too* much?

Reflection isn't my strong suit. People overthink everything. Amy's a perfect example of that. When you live in that kind of head space, it crowds out what's right in front of you. Decisions take energy, and that energy is what the body needs to fuel instinct.

I need to live in my body. Not want—*need*. Peak performance has no room for rumination.

And right now, I've no room for the wood Amy's introduced into my shower.

Some God-awful body wash that smells like cherries and expensive marketing campaigns is all I have to soap up with. Seventeen separate bottles of shampoo and conditioner litter every flat surface in the small shower. I grab one and finish up, replaying the scene with Amy.

When she walked in on me, I let her. I heard the knock. Knew the door was unlocked.

Wanted to see what she would do.

Now I know.

And I want to learn more, but with her naked, too.

My gym bag holds my dress pants, shirt, belt, and shoes, so preparing to go downstairs is a quick affair. I'm not putting on the suit James sent. There'll be no cameras, no pretense—I can just be me. Not Hamish McCormick, the football star. Not Hamish McCormick, the rising celebrity. No need to worry about the social media parasites always looking for the next clip to help their accounts go viral.

Amy's body loosened when I covered up. Mine loosens when I'm no longer under public scrutiny.

I'm barely down the stairs, headed toward the kitchen, when a tiny battalion of toddlers accosts me.

"Aymish!" Ellie screeches, immediately sitting on my foot, wrapping her legs around my ankle, hands at my knee. "Wanna ride!"

Andrew's twins decide to share my other foot, a scrum of little boys.

This is how I lurch into the kitchen.

"Who needs Six Flags when you can just ride Hamish?" Carol says dryly, looking at Amy as Shannon bites her lips to hold back laughter. Carol's younger boy, Tyler, sits at the table, drinking a glass of milk and looking sadly at the top of the fridge, where a black iPad rests.

One glance outside tells me the men are all hovering around the grill.

"I've got room for more," I say to Amy with a wink. In return, I get an eye roll, but she laughs.

"More! More!" one of the twins shouts. I lift my foot and shake it a bit, and they turn into a ball of giggles.

"This is better than any training," I announce, feeling a bit of a twinge in my hamstrings. "How much do they weigh?"

"About thirty-two pounds each," Amanda responds.

"Two stone, four pounds," I mutter.

"Fifteen kilos," Amy calculates instantly.

"Good fer a warm-up. Ma manager won't think it's enough, though."

"You get in trouble if you don't exercise?"

"If ma performance suffers, aye."

Jason appears at the sliding door with an old, scuffed football, the proper kind. I see Jason really does coach, and has played for quite some time. That's a well-loved ball.

Ellie peels off me and opens the door, condensation from cooking forming on the glass as a whuff of cold air chills the kitchen. The twins are right behind her, and my feet are light again.

Amy touches the back of my hand and nods toward the laundry room for me to follow, which I do.

Eagerly.

"I'm sorry about the bathroom incident. I really didn't know you were in there."

"It's nae problem. I get naked for a living. Might call me a professional," I add with a wink.

Her disgusted sigh fills me with joy.

"You're not making this easy."

"Making what easy?"

"I'm trying to be nice to you."

"Amy. Ma body is all over sports magazine covers. Half-dressed, and sometimes bare-arsed. I've nae problem with ye finding me naked."

"It was an accident!"

"And next time, maybe it wilna be."

"What's that supposed to mean?"

But she knows. She knows exactly what I'm saying, the air shifting between us. Following instinct means not letting words get in the way. My lungs know to fill and empty without me thinking about it. My hands and lips know where they need to go next.

But it's a full house, so there are no private moments.

"Hamish, can you hand me that case of pale ale?" Declan asks, Andrew behind him, the two looking serious.

I bend down, Amy shaking her head as she walks away. Moment missed.

"Here," I say to Declan, handing it off. "It's not cold."

"We'll chill it."

A glance at the clock tells me it's 1:30. "How long does this celebration go on?"

"Seven. Eight. First, they all scramble to cook a lot of food caterers could do almost as well. Then, they eat until they hate themselves. After that, Jason turns on football–"

I perk up.

Andrew laughs. "Not your kind. American football."

I groan.

"Then they keep eating pie, long after they should stop."

"And this is a beloved American day?"

Andrew nods, then turns to Declan. "How's that new project going?"

"Which one?"

"Tesla."

"I told them I would pay for the prototype, but no go. Elon wouldn't approve," Declan says to Andrew, who makes a disgusted face.

"I can't believe he wouldn't budge."

"Elon?" I ask. "Elon *Musk?*"

They both nod.

"Ye're trying to get involved with SpaceX?"

Both frown.

"No," Declan says with a long sigh. "Something even more inventive."

"A game changer, really," Andrew agrees with a nod.

"Something better than space travel? Must be amazing. What is it? A way to deliver health care to developing nations? Or, na–transporting sick children to hospitals?"

Now Declan's eyes cut away.

"Even better!" Andrew says enthusiastically.

"What is it, man? Spill it!"

"An espresso machine inside a Tesla," Shannon says, suddenly joining the conversation.

"That canna be right." I'm confused. "Ye want Elon Musk

to let ye put a coffee machine in a car? And ye consider it a game changer?"

"Worth a MacArthur Genius prize, huh?" Shannon cracks. Declan's jaw muscle goes as tight as ma Da's when someone English talks about Brexit.

"It would be! And it would be stocked with Grind It Fresh! coffee." Declan doubles down as Shannon goads him.

"Because everyone knows the only thing better than driving a Tesla is driving one while hopped up on caffeine." Her eyes twinkle.

"Right!" Andrew and Declan respond in unison.

"That reminds me. Any chance one of ye can drop me off at yer Da's house after all this?" I ask. "He was ma ride. I can take an Uber, of course, but–"

"We'll take you," Declan says, then leans in and whispers, "especially if you pretend you need to get back to Dad's early, so you can do your commercial thing with him."

"UP!" demands a small beastie suddenly at my feet. I look down to find one of the twins–I can't tell which is which–staring up at me, arms outstretched. All the toddlers have returned from their game outside. A pang of regret fills me.

Would have been fun to play with them.

I comply with the demand, but he begins wailing, clearly confused. All legs look like your grown-up's legs when you're the size of a footstool.

"Daddy!" he screeches, twisting in my arms like a greased pig as Andrew catches him.

Ellie runs over and offers herself in her cousin's place. I pick her up and start to put her on my shoulders, but realize that'll turn her head into a ceiling scraper. Instead, I opt for a piggyback ride and begin romping about the house.

"Piggyback! Piggyback!" she squeals.

As we canter past Marie, she raises her hand and declares, "Next!"

"You'll have to take a raincheck, Mom," Shannon calls

out from her spot in front of the oven, where she's peering at something through the glass. "Your leg is too compromised."

"My leg is fine. I'm healing."

As if to prove herself, she tries to stand.

"Good God, Marie, no!" Jason crashes through the crowd of people to reach her before she succeeds.

"Are they all this stubborn?" I ask Declan, whose eyes go hooded, a huff coming from his mouth.

"Are McCormicks competitive? Well, stubbornness is like that among the Jacoby women."

I bounce Ellie on my back. "Good luck wi' this one as a teen."

For the next ten minutes, I give the children rides. Carol's son Tyler comes over, giving me a look I know all too well. He's not a little boy, but definitely not a man. My youngest brother is the same age. Twelve is hard.

Even harder when you're different, I imagine.

I don't know the whole of it, but there's something about Tyler that's not quite typical. I've a teammate named Rocco who is similar. Quiet. Smart. But when he opens his mouth, not much makes sense. His feet, though–they make more sense than mine.

We all have our strengths, and the lucky ones find them. The rest flounder, never quite in sync with a world that punishes you for not being aligned.

"Ye want a ride?" I ask him. One corner of his mouth goes up, and Carol takes the iPad from his hand.

"Tyler! Is that where you were? Hiding in a bedroom on this thing? How'd you get it off the fridge?"

His eyes fly open. "Level 500!"

"I–" It's clear she wants to argue, but in the split second before saying the rest, decides it's not worth it. "No more iPad. Come play outside."

I motion to my back. "Want a turn?"

Jason's tending to the grill. The clock says it's nearing two p.m.

"Small crowd," Marie says sadly. "Just us. Terry's the only one missing now."

"When's he coming?" Amy asks her.

"Two."

"Are we eating early?"

"That would be great!" Declan says with an enthusiasm that makes me laugh.

Tyler is still contemplating my offer.

Then he looks at my feet.

"Wanna play?" he asks, heading for the door, eyes on Jason's shabby old ball.

Amy's watching us, her face kind, almost sad, as she looks at her nephew. I know that face. It's how I feel about people I love.

I love seeing her look at Tyler that way.

A piece of me wants her to look at me that way, too.

Amy

Hamish is staring at me.

Tyler's nonverbally begging Hamish to play with him, but the guy's too unaware to catch it. Being left out is the bane of Tyler's existence. He's smart and so good natured, but there are missing pieces in his repertoire that make it hard for him to connect.

And it breaks my heart.

"Tyler!" Hamish calls out suddenly, thumbing toward the back yard. "Spar wi' me."

"Spar?"

"Kick it."

Tyler races outside as if he's afraid Hamish will change his mind, but Hamish runs after him, acting like a gorilla, making all the toddlers laugh. It's cute and funny and–ah, no...

I cannot fall for him.

How can someone so shallow suddenly be so... interesting?

"You look like Elizabeth Bennet just after the turning point in *Pride and Prejudice*, when she's falling for Darcy," Shannon says to me as I stand at the window in the surprisingly empty kitchen. Declan, Andrew, Hamish, Dad, and all the kids–even Jeffrey–are outside playing soccer.

"Where's Carol?"

"Nice deflecting. She's in the shower."

"And Mom?"

A gentle snore makes us both look. She's conked out in her wheelchair.

"Thank you, God," I whisper.

"She hasn't been that bad."

"She was totally ready to launch herself at Hamish for a piggyback ride."

"She's not the only Jacoby woman ready to ride Hamish."

"*Shannon!*"

"What?"

"That sounds like something Carol would say."

"Carol's not here. I'm filling in for her. Like an understudy."

DING!

"If that's another woman–or man–with a dish, I'm going to scream," I say, taking the opportunity to evade her Elizabeth Bennet comment. As I pass the slider, Hamish grins at me, dripping with toddlers. They're hanging off him like a garland on a Christmas tree branch.

I can't help but grin back.

He winks.

My middle finger threatens to rise, the desire to flip him off stronger than expected. Why does he make me feel the highest highs and the lowest lows, the warmest connections and the deepest disgust?

"Hello," says Terry's bass voice at the front door. Of the three McCormick brothers, he's the one I've spent the least time with. He's the one I find most interesting, too.

He's holding a white cardboard box in one arm, and we hug awkwardly.

"I've brought you cannoli." He hands it to me.

"Cannoli?"

"From Mike's." Mike's is a famous Italian pastry shop in Boston's North End neighborhood.

"NO!"

"Yes."

I clutch the box like cradling a baby. "If I run upstairs, hide in a closet, and eat this whole thing, you'll keep my secret, right?"

"Only if I can join you." He peers around me. "Place is pretty empty. I can't be one of the first, can I?"

"They're all outside, playing soccer."

"That must mean Hamish is here."

"Yes. And Dad's grilling steaks."

"Steak *and* turkey? Fancy."

"Just steaks. We had an unfortunate turkey incident."

Terry's eyebrows shoot up, face filled with curiosity. He shrugs out of his coat and hangs it on a hook next to the door, and I see he's wearing a dress shirt and cable-knit sweater over his blue jeans, and brown leather loafers. I smile to myself; for Terry, from what I've seen, this is festive attire, his version of dressing up.

The squeals outside turn to sudden screams, including the men.

"There's a turkey in Grandpa's man cave!" Jeffrey yells, rushing into the house as Carol descends the stairs from the bathroom. She's beautifully made up, smiling at Terry, until her son's words register in her brain, smile going flat like a deflated balloon.

"What kind of a sex toy is a 'turkey,' and what have you done to Dad *this* time, Mom?" she bursts out. I instantly re-traumatize myself with the visual image of their bedroom when Dad called me from the hospital a whopping...

Two days ago? Has it really only been *two days?*

Time slows when your parents take a battering ram to your parasympathetic nervous system.

Mom startles from her nap and shouts, "ME?"

Just then, an enormous turkey–a live one–smashes into the sliding glass door. It reels back and flaps its wings. The thing is bigger than Ellie, who is in her dad's arms. Andrew's got both twins, and they're standing near the grill. Both men are watching the turkey with the deep caution of parents protecting the young.

Gobbling sounds come from the bird as it runs back to Dad's man cave, the door wide open.

"What happened?" Carol asks Jeffrey. "And where's Tyler?"

"In the man cave."

"Oh, my God!"

Before Carol can get to the door, Terry moves to the slider, opening it carefully. Dad's little converted shed is about thirty feet away. How fast can turkeys run? And can Terry run faster?

With a flick of his fingers, he motions to Declan and Andrew, who move like SWAT team members at a bust. They enter the house and hand the kids off to Shannon and Amanda.

The turkey pokes its head inside the man cave.

"Tyler's alone in there!" Carol starts to go outside, but Terry holds his palm up to her.

"I've got this," he whispers, moving slowly, step by step,

toward the man cave.

Dad is at the grill, still tending to the steaks but looking over his shoulder every three seconds.

"What's happening?" Mom asks as she begins wheeling herself to the sliders. Jeffrey pulls out his phone and holds it up, recording everything.

"This is going to make a *great* Tik Tok video," he says with an unmitigated glee that makes me fear for our nation's future.

"Your brother is out there alone with a turkey almost as big as he is ready to attack, and all you can think about is the viral video you'll get out of it?" Carol hisses.

"Yes."

She throws her hands up and watches Terry, one foot out the door, undecided.

"The beastie canna get oot o the bit," Hamish says, which makes even jovial Terry frown, eyes shifting to the right as he mentally translates.

"Turkey's stuck?" Terry asks.

"Aye. We need a plan," Hamish declares, and by *we*, he clearly means himself, Declan, and Andrew. They're now huddled together at the door, like a Navy SEAL team assigned to rescue a hostage.

To be fair, Tyler *is* being held hostage–by a turkey.

"We need a blanket," Hamish declares. "Throw it over the beast and toss the thing over the fence."

"You'll get torn apart by the claws," Andrew scoffs. He turns to Mom. "Does Jason have a gun?"

"WHAT?" every Jacoby female gasps.

"I'll take that as a no."

"I have a bow and arrow at home!" Jeffrey replies, suddenly eager, eyes lifted from his phone. "Mom, can I go home and get it?"

"No! Last time you used it, you hit the neighbor's dog!"

"I didn't actually pierce it."

As they argue, I take a few deep breaths and force myself to find my center.

Suddenly, I'm on the turkey's side.

Hamish, Andrew, and Declan disperse as I watch the poor thing. It's alone, trapped inside a fenced yard, scared, and doing whatever it can to find its way back to the familiar.

Hamish reappears with an old Patriots picnic blanket.

"Here we go."

Declan has a broom.

And Andrew? Andrew has a huge aluminum snow shovel he must have found in the garage.

This is why women live longer than men.

"What're you all doing?" I ask as they cluster near the sliding door, which is open enough for us to talk, but not so much that we're heating the great outdoors. They look like the cast of extras from the peasant scenes in *Shrek*.

As performed in community theater.

"Taking care of the turkey."

"You're insane."

"No, we're problem solving," Declan says, eyes narrow as he watches Terry moving closer to the so-called beast, spooking it enough that it changes direction, away from the open man cave door. Cautiously, Terry enters the shed and closes the door.

Carol lets out a huge breath of relief. Tyler's being protected.

"Where's Jason?" Mom asks, looking outside.

"At the grill."

"What? Why? He needs to come inside."

"He said he wasn't going to let twelve steaks and seven burgers go to waste. That the dog and cat had won the turkey battle, but he wouldn't let the turkey win the steak war."

"That makes no sense."

Declan looks sharply at Mom. "Nothing in this household ever does, Marie."

"Look," I explain to them all, forming my own plan. "Turkeys aren't exactly well endowed in the brain-cell department. Like Scottish footballers," I add.

"HEY!" Hamish snaps at me.

"The poor thing is lost. We just need to get it out the gate," I snap back.

"Gate?" all three men ask in the same tone.

My head explodes.

I'm out the door before anyone can stop me, marching to the left, where the gate in question is standing ajar. Someone left it open far enough for the stupid turkey to get in.

All I have to do is open it wider and shoo the thing out. Mr. Broom, Mr. Shovel, and Mr. Blanket can 'plan' all they want, but it takes a woman to get things *done*.

"Amy!" Dad is spearing steaks with a fork and loading a platter. "What are you doing?"

"Solving this!" I reach the gate and give it a push. The turkey is now banging against the back fence wall, increasingly agitated. It flaps its wings and jumps a few inches in the air, here and there. I know turkeys can fly, but they need a running start.

"AMY!" Hamish calls as I head toward the turkey, walking in a wide circle around it. If I run toward it, I'll scare it and it'll run away from me.

Like fifth grade recess and Tommy Liocci.

I look over at Hamish, whose eyes are worried. He has the blanket spread open, ready to throw over the turkey so he can carry it out. In the background, Chuffy has started barking nonstop.

"Even the bawtie canna scare it to the gate," Hamish says.

Terry slides open a window in Dad's man cave and shouts, "Tell Carol Tyler's fine. He wants her to know he's reached level 700 on his paper.io game."

Before I can do that, the turkey charges me.

And then Hamish does, too.

Everything goes dark as I'm covered, two hundred pounds of solid muscle flattening me onto the hard, frozen ground. One foot seems to be buried in a small pile of snow, and something thrashes above me. I'm on my back, completely covered by the blanket, but then the weight shifts and I inhale sharply.

And smell nothing but male power.

A bellow, a grunt, a warrior whoop, and Hamish shouts, "TEAMWORK!" as I struggle to get my hand free and pull the damn blanket off my face.

We're inches apart, mouths so close, I'm inhaling his warm breath.

Our eyes meet, locked in an endless gaze that penetrates me. The full weight of him no longer suffocates me. It holds me here, where I belong, under him, writhing and–

"The cock is gone," Hamish whispers.

"Excuse me?"

"The bird. The bird is gone."

I shove him off and stand, throwing the blanket at him.

"Why did you tackle me?"

"I covered ye with the blanket so the turkey wouldn't hurt ye. Then Declan cornered it with the broom, and Andrew scooped it out the gate ye opened. See? All four of us did it. Together."

"You tackled me, pinned me to the ground, and smothered me!"

"Aye. But yer safe now. And ye're welcome."

"*What?* You expect me to *thank you* for that? When I was the only one with the common sense to just open the gate and let the damn bird out?"

"Ye were charging a wild turkey, Amy. Nae common sense in that."

"DINNER!" Carol calls. Terry and Tyler emerge from the man cave and everyone heads into the house.

Show over.

9
———

Hamish

The dinner table is full of mystery.

"What's this?" I ask Carol. She's to my right, Amanda to my left, and Amy across from me. I'm staring at a jiggly bowl of something burgundy colored.

"Cranberry sauce."

"Sauce? It's no' a liquid."

"Right. It's a gelatinous mass of yummy goodness," she expands.

"Why does it have rings along the edges and look like someone dumped it out o' a tin?"

"Because they did."

"Heard of them, but never seen them. Cranberries are like gooseberries?"

"Sort of. They're native to Massachusetts. It's a big thing here."

Never afraid to try something new, I take a spoonful.

Amy promptly offers me a different bowl, also burgundy, but not jelly.

"Try this. The real stuff."

"Is this the kind ye like, Amy?"

She makes a face. "I hate cranberry sauce."

"I thought Carol said it's a big thing here?"

"That's just it–it's been forced on me for years."

"And ye never developed a taste fer it?"

"Constant pressure just made me hate it even more."

It's a little hard to breathe as I hear those words. I don't know why.

"And this?" I point to a casserole dish filled with small chunks of toasted bread.

"Stuffing. It's bread and herbs you put inside the turkey when it bakes."

"Aye. I know what it is. I thought the beasties took off wi' the turkey. Surely ye didna rescue the stuffing from them?"

"No. You can bake it in a separate dish, too, and then it's actually called dressing." Amy turns toward the kitchen. "We have three different kinds. Regular, chestnut, and oyster."

Carol shudders. "Oyster dressing. Only a monster would do that."

"Hey!" Jason comes in from the kitchen, holding two little pieces of bone in his hands. "We couldn't save the meat, but I did find the wishbones." He sets them on the bread plate at his place. "A reminder of good intentions."

He picks up the platter of steaks and begins dispensing them onto plates. No buffet style here. This is a big family, crammed around a dining table and a folding table covered in matching tablecloths.

Jason starts to sit, then changes his mind and goes into the living room.

"Dashing through the snow…" Christmas music fills the air.

Half the table groans.

Half the table cheers.

Ye can guess which family does which.

"The Boston Pops!" Shannon exclaims, delighted.

"Can't you at least wait until after dinner to start?" Declan asks his father-in-law, who shakes his head, grinning madly.

"It's my one pleasure this year," Marie declares. She's sitting next to Jason, who is at the head of the table. I count fifteen of us: Amy, Terry, Carol, Tyler, Jeffrey, Declan, Shannon, Ellie, Amanda, Andrew, Charlie, Will, Jason, and Marie. And me.

Large enough for good conversation and fun.

Small enough to feel like you're one of the family.

"A toast!" Jason calls out. Everyone at the table lifts their glass, except for Amanda and Andrew, who are performing Olympic-level wrestling moves to prevent Will from eating a container of salt and Charlie from using the gravy as finger paint.

I reach for my wine glass. A mix of reds and whites dots the long table. While I'm normally not one for wine, I'm following their lead.

"To firsts. Hamish's first Thanksgiving, Marie's first year not doing the cooking, Amy will be our first child with a master's degree soon–"

I look at Amy, who smiles at me with a blindly beautiful grin of pure joy.

"And to our first steak dinner on turkey day."

"And to Declan, Andrew, and Hamish for getting the live turkey out of the back yard!" Marie adds.

Amy's face tightens. Damn.

I hold my glass up and look at her. "To Amy, the only one of the lot of us wi' the common sense to open the gate."

Everyone turns to her in smiling acknowledgment. Her grateful eyes meet mine across the table, and an instant flash of having her under me in the backyard makes me want more.

Cheers go all around as we take our sips, then go back to passing dishes. Filling my belly might get rid of the hollow feeling I have when I look at her now. If that'll work, then I've plenty of food here to do it with.

"Speaking of firsts, Hamish, you should come to our Yankee swap this year," Carol says.

"And what is a Yankee swap?" I don't even want to guess, with this family. If Marie broke her leg in a sex swing, what kind of "swap" is Carol talking about?

"Here," Amy says to me loudly, no one answering my question, pointing to a dish that looks like orange mashed potatoes dotted with clumps of white icing. "Yam bake. Try some."

I take a spoonful and a taste.

"What's the white stuff?" I ask. It's sweet and gooey, with a texture that's nothing like icing.

"Marshmallow."

Everyone seems to be loading their plate as if they only get one chance, so I do the same. No one's settling in, though, or going quiet.

What's a family gathering like this about if not a wee bit more merriment?

I clear my throat. "Unless Jason, as the man o' the house, is intending to do it, I'd like to say grace."

Everyone pauses, a slow smile creeping along Marie's lips.

Jason nods my way, giving permission. Without my saying a word, everyone slowly reaches for the hands of the person next to them, the wee twin boys doing it so sweetly, big eyes on me and their Mum, everyone suddenly so respectful.

Back home, one of my brothers would be shoving a forkful in his face, getting a well-deserved whack on the back of his neck by Da, so this is quite different.

I say the prayer:

. . .

Some hae meat an canna eat,
  And some wad eat that want it;
  But we hae meat, and we can eat,
  And sae the Lord be thankit.

Jason looks astonished, eyebrows up, but Marie starts clapping.

"Perfect! So true. This might be the first Thanksgiving in my entire life where we don't have turkey," she says, pointedly glaring at Carol, Shannon, and Amy, whose eyes are suddenly anywhere but on their mum, "but we do have meat we can eat."

Carol's shoulders go tight. She's clearly worried about what he mother will say next.

"So let's eat our meat and enjoy it!" Marie holds her wine glass aloft, and we all follow, glasses clinking, the children reaching for them, Charlie's fat fingers dipping into Andrew's beer, the wee laddie too fast for his father, licking the drink off his own hand with a sucking motion, like he was at his mother's breast.

And then we all feast, the steak perfectly seasoned and cooked for such an impromptu production. There's surprisingly little talking, considering this crowd. Marie's a talker, but she's been muted more than usual today.

For which I'm grateful.

"How is everything?" Amy asks politely as I put a forkful of yams in my mouth, a full taste this time. It's sweet, with a burnt-sugar caramel taste that catches me off guard.

I moan.

A sultry smile spreads across her face, cheeks flushing with a heat I can almost feel across the table. Our eyes lock and I stop chewing, time stopped between us.

All I want is to touch her.

Everything I need is right there.

"Hamish likes something!" Marie calls out, bending forward in her seat to catch my attention.

Amy's eyes tear away and she grabs her wine glass, taking a gulp.

"Yam... mmmm." My body buzzes as I swallow.

"That's Liz Tayton's signature dish. She uses maple sugar in it. Not maple syrup, maple sugar."

"And a hint of clove," I add.

"Yes! You have a good palate," Marie replies.

"When I taste something, its secrets are all revealed to me."

At that, Amy looks up at me sharply, the pulse at her throat visible with the open neckline of her dress.

Bzzzz

My phone turns feral in my pocket, buzzing over and over, and I have no choice but to look.

It's Jody.

Call me immediately.

I frown. It's a holiday. No offices are open. Must be something to do with a deal, but it would be rude to interrupt this fine meal for a business call. Nothing's a true emergency.

Naw. The wine, the food, the crazy day has me wanting more of this, and less of *that*.

I power off my phone.

Two full plates later, I'm stuffed.

"Pie!" Carol calls out. "I'll go make the whipped cream now. But someone has to help with dishes." She looks pointedly at her eldest son, who suddenly turns to Declan and asks him how business is going.

"I'll help," I announce, standing.

Everyone goes silent.

"You'll help with the dishes?" Amy squeaks out, clearly surprised.

"Aye. Of course." I walk over to the kitchen door, rolling up my sleeves.

"*Ow!*" Andrew bursts out from behind me. Then: "What was *that* for?"

"Looks like the Scottish McCormicks trained *their* kids to be helpful," Amanda hisses at her husband.

"Oh, come on."

"A real man does dishes."

"No. A real man hires people to do dishes." I turn to find Andrew waving Jeffrey over, a twenty-dollar bill in his hand.

Declan stands, sighing. "Fine. I'll help."

Andrew reluctantly joins his brother and me as Amy goes out of her way to find every dirty dish in the house, including a few that I think were under houseplants. The pile is enormous. I tackle a large platter.

Andrew pulls out his phone. "Let me get Gina on this."

"We can do that? Get our executive assistants to help?" Declan asks, reaching into his pocket.

"You can try." Andrew starts scrolling, then pauses. "I know Gina has a line. This might cross it."

"You're respecting that your executive assistant has a line? Aww, little bro. You're maturing. That's so cute."

"Says the guy who has his EA make a delivery to his mother-in-law's house on Thanksgiving."

"No, Dad had Dave deliver." Declan frowns. "Hold on. How did Dad do that? Dave works for me?"

Shannon pats his arm. "Don't worry about Dave. He's shrewd. I'm sure James paid him an obscene amount."

CLAP CLAP!

We all look into the dining room. Marie surveys the long table, napkins left beside empty plates and half-filled glasses, crumbs and spills and candle wax drips on the tablecloth. She smiles just like my own mother does after a big family gathering, a wistful twist of the mouth that only someone with decades of memories can produce. She isn't just looking at this year's table.

She's seeing all the tables of all the years that came before it.

"Christmas decorations!" she announces to a chorus of groans from everyone except me and the wee toddlers. Even Tyler does it, though he looks a bit mystified, as if he's not quite in on a joke everyone else understands.

Suddenly, my cousins disappear.

"Ye're verra excited to help wi' those decorations," I tease, until I realize why they've gone into the living room.

A sports announcer's voice fills the room.

"Ach, God, no," I call out. "No' that shite!"

American football.

I'd rather be elbow deep in dirty dishwater.

Amy

Nothing about this day has gone the way I expected.

There was none of the back-breaking cooking that we dreaded.

No one ate a single bite of turkey.

We fought off a live turkey in the yard.

And I saw Hamish McCormick's, er... todger.

In all its glory.

But none of that is what I'm talking about.

What I expected least, and surprised me most, is this:

Hamish McCormick is a more nuanced person than I gave him credit for.

He's still an ass, but he's a complex, layered ass, with some really sweet, protective qualities thrown in there.

Maybe I really should give him a chance.

Dad, Declan, and Andrew are all pretending to help with

the Christmas decorations, but they're yelling at the television as if that'll actually help the Lions win.

It's a family tradition. Every year on Thanksgiving, we all root for the poor Detroit Lions because they're always there. Except for Tyler, who roots for the referee.

We're a family who believes in the underdog, even when it's unbelievably impractical. If Mom and Dad have taught us nothing else, it's to practice radical optimism.

Shannon and Amanda are on little-kid patrol. Mom is snoring lightly on the recliner, a pose Dad usually assumes. Jeffrey and Tyler are silent faces illuminated by blue screens. The only ones actually decorating are Terry and Carol.

Hamish is doing all the dishes by himself.

And me?

I'm eating a pile of whipped cream with a slice of pumpkin pie buried under it.

For the next ten minutes, I am pie. Nothing but pie and whipped cream. I suppose there is a point at which the human stomach will actually split open from eating too much pumpkin pie with whipped cream, but two (and a half) slices isn't quite at that point.

I do loathe myself, but that's part of the tradition.

Mom, refreshed, moves over to the small chair on casters that she begged Dad to pull out, so she can maneuver better in the kitchen. Shannon's cuddling on the couch with a very-asleep Ellie in her arms, Shannon's hand smoothing her little girl's dark, silky hair.

Football on the television. Too much dessert. Christmas decorations. The sound of Jeffrey and Tyler, now playing with the twins, laying out Dad's old Lionel train set. This is what holidays are really about.

Family.

Home.

Comfort.

"Hey! Amy!" Hamish walks over, holding one of the two

wishbones Dad retrieved from the stolen turkey carcasses. "I've a bone here I want ye to pull."

And assholes.

"I've seen your bone already, Hamish. I'm fine."

"Ye must be more than fine after a look at *ma* bone."

"I'm all twitterpated."

"Ye took photos to put on Twitter? Amy, I'm flattered."

"Just when I start to think that maybe I'm not giving you the benefit of the doubt, you prove me right."

"I hear it's a competition," he says, holding up the wishbone. "Whoever gets the V wins."

His grin makes me wet *and* furious.

"It's basic physics. No skill involved."

"Like yer first time having sex."

I grab one end of the wishbone and yank.

"I win," I tell him, tossing my piece at his chest. "I got the V."

It bounces off him and onto the floor.

"V for virgin?" he purrs.

It would be easy, so easy. Too easy–to throw myself into his arms, let him kiss me, let him touch me, let him do, well...

Everything.

As my cool, rational mind tries to explain to all my hot-blooded parts why that's a very, very bad idea, Mom interrupts us.

"Hamish! Did you see the mistletoe? You could give someone a lively Scottish kiss." Mom winks at him as she grabs the backs of chairs, then the edge of the table, to scooch closer to us.

He looks appalled. Good.

"Why would I do that to someone here?"

"Because it's tradition!"

"Ye crazy Americans go around breaking each other's noses under the mistletoe?"

"What? No!"

"That's what a Scottish kiss is, Marie!"

"How is that remotely romantic?"

"Yer proving ma point!"

"How about you just give Amy a regular kiss, then? That's what mistletoe is for, right?"

"MOM!" Carol shouts from the kitchen. "I think I ruined the whipped cream."

"I thought you already made a batch!"

"It's gone. This is the second one, and it's turned to butter."

Mom begins inching herself toward Carol, calling, "That's the good stuff from Mapleline Farm! Don't ruin it!"

Hamish looks at the sprig of white berries and green leaves hung from the living room door frame. He's almost at eye level with it, tall and powerful.

"We have the same tradition back home, ye know. Invented it."

"The Scots invented mistletoe?"

"Nae. The tradition, though. Goes back to Druids and pagans and all that." He gives me a jaunty grin. "Mistletoe is a fertility symbol."

I snort.

"It makes me feel like I'm home." His head tilts, eyes opening slightly, green and lush and strong. He's an ass sometimes, but once again, there's more depth than I expected.

Plus, who gets invited to a huge family gathering and volunteers to do all the dishes? Carol told me earlier he was a keeper, and I'm starting to agree.

Maybe. Kinda. Sorta.

Before I can stand on tiptoe to give him a quick kiss on the cheek, he's bending down, his hand below my shoulder blade, warm and strong, his lips touching mine. The brush of his warm mouth is sweet.

And then, suddenly, it isn't.

It's hot. Wet. All consuming. No tongue, no breach, no vulgar display of claiming. Hamish is kissing me respectfully, but he's kissing me with the full attention of a man who means it.

My hand goes to his chest, meeting rock-hard muscle, the beat of his heart quickening under my touch.

Then, air.

Cold air.

"Now, that wasna so bad, was it?"

He smiles, questions in his eyes, but I don't know exactly which ones he's asking.

If I knew, I'd answer.

The television broadcast changes from the game to sports news.

"That's Hamish!" Jeffrey squeals in a little-kid voice, looking at the screen. "Why are you on television?"

Hamish freezes in place, spine stretching up, making him impossibly tall. His wide shoulders are tensing, eyes filling with...

Trepidation?

"Jody!" he hisses, feeling in his pockets for his phone.

"Jody?"

"Ma agent. He was texting me at dinner and I ignored him."

"*Shhhhhh!*" Dad raises the television volume. "Let's see what the news is about Hamish! Maybe a big endorsement contract?"

Something's wrong, and I don't know what it is, but a cold dread fills my stomach. Whatever's about to flash across that screen won't be good.

Won't be good at all.

"Scottish footballer Hamish McCormick is in the head-lines again, and this time it's not about Cup matches or endorsement contracts. The noted playboy was caught on camera in a scandalous sex tape–"

"Uhhh…" Dad starts as Declan and Andrew lean in, reaching for the remote to turn the sound up further.

"–sleeping with the daughter of the AFC Dunsdill team owner."

"*Ohhhhh,*" Declan and Andrew say in unison, as if Hamish had made a bad play, reacting like fans do when players screw up.

Which he did.

"I… That's…There's… I can explain," Hamish stammers, but a grainy video clip makes it clear I'm not the only person who's going to see him naked today.

Dad abruptly turns off the television as Declan and Andrew groan, and not because they're upset by what Hamish has done, but because they want the juicy details.

"Well," Dad says slowly. "Anyone up for a good game of Scrabble?"

"Sure," I say, moving away from Hamish as fast as possible. "What's the letter score for the word manwhore?" I pronounce it with a Scottish accent, drawing out the *hoooooor* sound.

Hamish closes his eyes and has the decency to blush.

"I deserve that."

"You deserve worse. Who sleeps with their boss's daughter?"

Declan points to Hamish from behind him as Andrew snorts.

"I would try to explain, but it's clear nothing I say would matter," Hamish says in a formal voice that almost – *almost* – sounds contrite.

"You made sports headlines on Thanksgiving day, on national television, Hamish. That speaks for itself."

"Ye believe everything ye see on the telly?"

"That video didn't leave much to the imagination, Hamish," Dad says in a choked voice.

"It did for me! You were standing in the way, Jason, and I missed all the good stuff!" Mom complains.

Hamish lets out a sigh, then reaches for my arm. I shake him off. He leans in.

"A word wi' ye in private?"

"I know what you do to women in private."

"With," he says, over-enunciating the word. "*With* women."

Some cold piece of me hardens even more, the memory of that kiss just moments ago tainted by the sports news scandal. Why should I delude myself into thinking I'm special to Hamish?

I'm not.

And if I'm going to fall for someone, that's a pretty low bar for expectations.

"Let me be crystal clear. One hundred percent transparent. Blisteringly blunt." I tap his chest with my fingertips, then touch my throat. "There is no way I will ever, ever sleep with you."

He starts to interrupt. I cover his mouth with my hand, our eyes meeting, his going wide.

"Mmmph."

"I mean it, Hamish. So stop the flirting. The double entendres. The sexual innuendoes. All of it. You really are the polar opposite of what I want in a man, so stop wasting your energy and my good will. Give it up."

He touches the backs of my fingers and I lift them from his smooth, recently-shaved face, the textured warmth of his skin sending more ripples of emotion through me that I have to fight.

I brace myself for his cocky response.

Mom and Carol start arguing in the background over whether this year's Thanksgiving really was better than the way Mom does it. Ellie's found a scrunchie and is trying to put Chuffy's ears in a ponytail. Amanda and Shannon are huddled on the couch, whispering like fiends, which means they're talking about sex.

Dad really did pull out the Scrabble game, which brings Jeffrey and Tyler to the dining table, leaving Declan and Andrew to manage the twins, while Terry searches through yet another box of decorations, setting small porcelain figurines in all the wrong places.

And all I can focus on is Hamish. Everything else fades away. I hate him even more for really being what I thought all along, but more than that?

It hurts to have seen that there *is* more in there. It's just covered by all the rest. And by "the rest," I mean a televised sex scandal.

That's a big, big, "the rest."

"I think I rather like this strange holiday, Amy," he murmurs, though his face is closed off more.

"Mmm."

"But I liked it better when ye pulled ma wishbone."

I hit him, hard, trying to make him flinch but, dammit, he doesn't.

"You are a disgusting pig."

"And yer even more bonnie when ye're pissed at me. Which is how I like it."

Then the jerk wanders off, sauntering with that casual, cocky grace guys have when they know you're staring at their fine, sculpted-marble ass.

Which I definitely wasn't.

Because Hamish McCormick is never, ever going to get anywhere near me again.

Especially not my mouth.

SNEAK PEEK OF SHOPPING FOR A HIGHLANDER, THE NEXT HAMISH AND AMY BOOK:

I'm a professional chickenblocker.

Except 'chicken' is a euphemism.

I get paid to follow an infuriating womanizing sports hero troglodyte who thinks rules are for other people and that *my* pants are the next pair he's getting into.

Dream on.

Bet *your* first professional job didn't involve babysitting an extremely hot, muscle-bound fooball-playing Scottish Highlander with an ego the size of his kilt and a libido bigger than his...well...

Chicken.

Keeping football (that's soccer to us Americans) player Hamish McCormick out of scandals while he does product endorsement campaigns is my mission.

No problem.

Until Hamish decides *I'm* his next scandal.

And maybe more....

Shopping for a Highlander is an enemies-to-lovers, slow burn romance that opens with a surprise kiss and ends with a happily ever after. This sports comedy spinoff in the *New*

York Times-bestselling *Shopping for a Billionaire* world contains no actual chickens, but it has plenty of changing room scenes, a fake relationship, very real banter, and more. You do not have to have read the previous books in this world, though after you read about Amy and Hamish, you'll want to. ;)

Chapter One

Amy

I am standing here in my graduation gown as I graduate with my MBA from UMASS Amherst, with photographers snapping pictures like crazy, and Hamish McCormick's tongue is in my mouth.

I realize this is a problem half the women in the world would love to have. He's a world-famous Scottish soccer – sorry, *football* to everyone except Americans – player and my sister is married to his cousin, the billionaire.

Given the fact that Hamish is kissing me in front of my date, though, it's a little awkward.

"Ahem," Davis says, scratching his temple and adjusting his glasses using polite, understated throat techniques to get Hamish off me. Subtlety doesn't work on Hamish, though. This kiss is anything but subtle. Pretty sure you need a crowbar to pry him off me.

Or me off him. The difference between who is kissing whom was lost long ago.

I see Davis out of the corner of my eye, and I'm about to shove this two-hundred-pound sack of hard muscle and over-confident heat off of me and slap him, but sweet merciful deity I swear Hamish's lips have some kind of magic potion on them that renders me spellbound.

No kiss has ever tasted like this.

Other than the last kiss from him, six months ago, under the mistletoe at my family's Thanksgiving celebration.

You know. The kiss that happened right before news broke about Hamish screwing his team owner's daughter after their sex tape was leaked to the media.

Yeah. That kiss. *That* kiss tasted like this.

We're all wearing burgundy graduation gowns and as I pull away, Hamish tracks with me, his hands flattening against my shoulder blades, his tongue soft and discreet, caressing me like I'm naked in bed and we have an acre of mattress to explore.

He can round my Cape of Good Hope anytime. He can be the Ponce deLeon to my virgin territory.

"Hamish!" My mother's shrill voice cuts through this tormenting fantasy come to life. "How wonderful of you to stop by for Amy's graduation ceremony!" She's grinning up at him, arms wide in anticipation of a hug.

Then she looks at my date. "Oh, hi, Davis. I didn't know you'd be here?" The uptick in her voice turning that into a question shows that even my mother, who is the embodiment of the word *awkward*, realizes this is a social mess.

Air. Suddenly, I can breathe again. There is entirely too much air in the world, and I'm sucking all of it in at the same time. A single breath becomes the atmosphere.

"Marie," Hamish says, giving Mom a big hug, one she enjoys as her eyes close and she squeezes him with genuine affection. Mom's proud of me, for sure, but it's the human connection at big events that she enjoys more.

"I hate to hug and run," she says, "but Jason's waiting for me in the car. He'll be so sad to have missed you." Mom skitters off, leaving me with a million questions.

"So guid to see you again, Amy. Ma congratulations." Hamish is staring down at me, ginger hair clipped short on the sides and back, but longer across his forehead, hanging in waves so insolent they deserve a spanking.

Why am I thinking about *spankings*?

"Amy." Davis is using his serious voice. The one he uses when he thinks I'm being ridiculous. We've only been dating for three weeks, and he already as a Ridiculous Voice.

You know what Davis *doesn't* have?

Magic potion lips.

"Yes. Oh! Right. Davis, this is Hamish. Hamish, meet Davis."

Hamish reaches for Davis's hand and wrings it like he's working out a muscle spasm in poor Davis's forearm. I didn't know a shoulder joint could turn in so many directions.

But Davis gamely tries to match Hamish's strength, despite being eight inches shorter, a good forty pounds lighter, and really, viscerally not wanting to be touched by the man I've complained about during my entire friendship – and now romantic relationship – with Davis.

"Hi," he says, eyes going narrow. "*The* Hamish?"

I get a saucy look and a half-grin from the man who just imprinted his taste on me. "Aye."

"What are you doing here?" I ask, a rising anger starting in my toes, creeping up like a tingle that has no intention of stopping until it gets to the crown of my head. "I'm – I'm graduating. This is my ceremony. Of all the places in the world where you could turn up, why here? Why now?"

"And why kiss Amy like that?" Davis's worlds hold a challenge in them, his dark, thick beard hiding how clenched his jaw is. Horn-rimmed glasses encircle dark brown eyes that crowd each other. He's wearing a graduation gown, like me, but dark, shined dress shoes, men's wingtips that signal he's serious about business.

I'm stuck in four-inch heels because Mom insisted.

"Ach. The kiss? That was a bet."

"A bet!" I gasp.

A short, compact man with the busy air of a reincarnated hummingbird appears behind Hamish. "Short" might be an unfair description, because he's taller than me, and about Davis's height, but compared to Hamish, every man is short.

"Saw it," he says, clapping Hamish on the back, his accent English, but I can't place it. "Jesus, Hamish, you really can find someone to kiss whenever and wherever you want." He slips Hamish something, hand to hand. "You win."

"You arrogant piece of work," I say, moving closer to Hamish, truly ready to slap him. "You bet on me?"

"Ye made it easy."

"I am not easy!" Out of the corner of my eye, I see Shannon approach, her face changing to confusion as she spots Hamish. It's impossible to miss him, a redhead standing a good four inches above most people in the crowd.

Big, burly, with a model's good looks and an Olympian's athletic body, he's the face of more and more sports products, and in America, nothing makes you more famous than hawking a consumer product.

The more popular, the better.

"Never said ye were. Just that ye made it easy, pet."

"Don't call me that!" I shout.

Shannon catches up to us, moving next to me just as my date does, too.

Davis reaches for my arm, hand on my elbow, leaning in. He whispers, "Don't make a scene."

Something in Hamish's expression hardens, a microscopic shift I now realize, with a sinking feeling, that I do notice.

Because I do track him.

"I'm not making a scene." I point to Hamish. "He started it."

A lascivious grin from Hamish turns into something deeper as Shannon frowns.

My sister and I are nothing alike. Shannon has no ambition. Happy in life, she's all about her close circle of family and friends. I don't mean that she isn't a hard worker – she is – or that she doesn't have good ideas – she does.

It's the drive that Shannon lacks.

Marrying Declan McCormick, the billionaire's son of self-made billionaire James McCormick, founder of Anterdec, one of the biggest corporations in Boston, was Shannon's smartest move in life.

Of course, love had everything to do with it.

She's Vice President of Grind It Fresh!, the regional chain of coffee shops that Declan bought for her as a wedding gift (hello, billionaire husband…), but she's slowly reducing her hours at their company because she wants to be at home with my niece.

And soon, I suspect, more kids.

Shannon's here to support me on my big day, a day that celebrates drive and determination, but she's also here to be my friend.

Something just set her off.

It takes a *lot* to pis off Shannon.

"Davis," she says through gritted teeth, moving from happy energy to seething contempt so quickly I do a double take to make sure I haven't confused her for our other sister, Carol. "What did you just say to Amy?"

We're standing in a cluster – me, Shannon, Davis, Hamish, and Hamish's friend, who has his hands on his hips and twitches like a little kid stuck in a dentist office waiting room.

Hamish watches Shannon with glee.

"Aye, Davis. What did ye just say to Amy?"

"I told her not to make a scene," he says confidently, looking around. "You, of all people, should understand," he adds with a quiet grin to my sister, expecting an ally.

"Me? I should understand?" she says back with a deadly, flat expression. Whoa. Declan's taught her a few tricks.

"You're experienced in business. You're a McCormick. Making scenes leaves the impression that one is less stable."

One of Hamish's eyebrows flies up, tongue trolling under his lower lip.

"Who would think that, Davis?" Shannon asks with a head tilt he erroneously takes for agreement.

And suddenly, I get it.

Internal groaning commences.

Because Davis looks nothing like my sister's ex-fiancee, Steve Raleigh. Speaks nothing like him. Is the polar opposite of Steve in so many ways – politics, food choices, movie selections, life goals.

But he's tone policing me. Telling me not to stand up for myself.

And in that sense, he's no different.

Which makes this whole mess worse than I thought.

Because now I have to *thank* Hamish for kissing me.

Hamish

I'd have kissed her without Harry's stupid bet, but it sweetened the pot.

Amy's mouth was more than sweet enough.

Was it brash? Aye. Should I have done it? Nae, but she kissed me right back, so fiercely and with an enthusiastic all-in that made it clear I wasn't breaking any of her boundaries, so I did it.

And her twee boyfriend tried to step in.

I've nothing against the man. Or, at least, I didn't.

Until he made that comment.

What's wrong with making a scene? Scenes are just the result of being yourself. If other people watch, then that's on them.

Davis hasn't answered Shannon's question about who would think that someone's unstable for making a scene.

"And what's wrong with being perceived as unstable?" I

ask, unable to help myself. "Is there a crown ye earn at the end o' yer life for being stable? Sounds boring, Davis."

He snorts and shakes his head, but says nothing.

Which means he's either a coward or a prig.

Or both.

Shannon gives Amy a sad smile and says, "Code Raleigh." I've no idea what that means, but it can't be good, given the way Amy's face falls.

Tension wears on people in different ways. There's nothing quite like the stress of losing a match, the post-match changing room a sweaty, oily soup of disappointment and blame.

Some people can't handle direct confrontation. They live in the margins, passive-aggressive and snide, unable to say what they mean and mean what they say.

I'm not one of those people.

"I think," I say, loud on purpose, turning a few heads, "that we're here to celebrate Amy's great accomplishment. I never finished college, ye know."

Something gleams in Davis's narrowed eyes. Amy moves an inch or two away from him, the movement subtle. Shannon takes a deep breath and searches the crowd.

"Went for a year, but football was ma future," I continue.

"The best future!" Harry calls out with a clap. I'd damn near forgotten he was with me.

"Why are you here, Hamish?" Amy asks softly, looking up at me with doe eyes. Vulnerable and quieter, she's more grounded. Less angry.

Searching for answers.

"It's a long, funny story, but it boils down to girls and football."

Her face sours. "Of course it does. Your two favorite subjects."

Harry barks out a laugh and gives me a hearty clap on the back.

"Nae, no' this time," I say with a wink. "Literally girls and football." I let out a sigh. "Fine. Girls *soccer*. There's a big clinic at Amherst College here in town, and I've been coaching the nine year olds, along wi' being part o' the marketing campaign."

"That almost sounds altruistic."

"Those little lassies are vicious. I've nae skin left on ma shins." I shake a leg for good measure, and she bursts out laughing.

"That's because you're shite at football, Hamish," Harry adds, laughing with such joy that even Shannon and Amy join in. Harry's naught but a bundle of overagitated nerves, but he's got a goalie's mind.

Throw yourself in front of whatever obstacle life sends and head butt it right back.

Davis' phone buzzes. He looks at the screen. "My parents are wondering where I am," he says to Amy. "I'll catch you later."

"Mmm," she says as he gives her hand a light squeeze, then wanders off, her eyes following him, face turning into something between a wince and a reckoning.

"Mmm," Shannon says, one corner of her mouth turned tight, her and Amy watching Davis as he leaves.

"You're right," Amy says in horror. "I can't believe I didn't notice it before."

"They're subtle, these men. Steve was like that. Frog in a pot."

"Frog in a what?" I ask, moving closer to them as Harry wanders off toward the toilets.

"You know the old adage? How people would never jump into a pot of boiling water, but put a frog in a pot of cold water and slowly turn up the temperature..."

"Aye. Yer saying Davis is like that wi' Amy? Only the water is his need to tell her what to do?"

"Yes."

"And how would ye know this, Shannon?"

"Because my fiancee before I met Declan was a controlling, arrogant, manipulative jerk."

"Let me guess – with an MBA?"

"Mmm."

"Glad ye found ma cousin, then. He might be a bit closed off, but he's no asshole."

"A ringing endorsement," I hear from behind us as Declan, holding wee Ellie on one hip, finds our little group. "What the hell are you doing here, Hamish?"

"Teaching a girl's football clinic in town. Marie found out and texted me. Asked me to stop by."

Amy's expression makes it clear the puzzle pieces fell into place and Marie's due for a tongue lashing later.

"You coming over to Marie and Jason's house for dinner?" Declan asks.

"Nae. Have to get back to the camp. But thank ye." I eye Amy. "Could have been fun."

Harry comes back. "Your family just keeps expanding!" he says as Declan puts Ellie down.

"That's how family is, right?" I say, ruffling Ellie's dark hair.

"Hamish," she says, her little toddler language skills expanding, the H at the beginning of my name distinct now. "Wanna race?"

Last Thanksgiving, I was stuck in this country and spent a crazy day with the Jacoby family at their house in Mendon. Racing little Ellie on the sidewalk was one of the highlights.

Chasing a live turkey out of their backyard was not.

"Not now, lass. But soon."

Harry tugs on my shirt. "Gotta go, Hamish. You tapped me out of my twenty and the camp dinner starts soon."

Amy's face hardens at the mention of the bet.

"By the way, Hamish," she says loudly, clearly not worried about making scenes now. "Thank you for kissing me."

Shannon and Declan give us quite the look.

"Yer thanking me now? I thought ye were about to slap me."

I'll take the expression of gratitude if it comes with another kiss, though.

"If you hadn't done that, Davis wouldn't have gotten jealous, and we wouldn't have learned he's a Code Raleigh."

A furious look fills in Declan's features. "Steve Raleigh? He's here? What's he doing now?"

"No, not Steve," Shannon assures him. "Amy saw a different side of Davis today."

"Oh." Declan shrugs. "Never met him before until today. He seemed fine. Uptight, but fine. Networked with me."

Pain fills Amy's eyes, which she closes slowly, taking a long, deep breath.

"We were friends for a year. Then we were assigned to a team for a group project. The one we turned in right before Thanksgiving. When we came back from break, he hung out with me more. Asked me out a few weeks ago. I've been on guard against people using me for my connections to you," she says looking at Declan. "But I thought Davis wasn't like that."

"We always do, don't we?" Shannon says with great sympathy. "We always think they're not like that, because we would never pick someone who is 'like that.'"

"And then I did." The words out of Amy's mouth pierce me.

Make me not want to be 'like that.'

Because I damn well am not.

"Is it too much to ask to find a guy who doesn't need my star to shine a little less so his can seem brighter?" Amy goes on, gutting me. She's saying it to Shannon, but she's also saying it to the world.

"No," Declan answers firmly. "It's not too much to ask. Guys like Davis are everywhere in business."

"They're in sports, too," I add. "I'm nae one o' them, but there's plenty."

Amy looks up and me, her face serious, studying me.

"You may be a manwhore, and a playboy, and a cocky jerk, but I will give you that, Hamish: you're not someone who needs to diminish a woman in order to feel better about yourself."

I flatten my hand against my chest. "Did hell freeze over, Amy? Because I believe ye just paid me a compliment."

"Don't get used to it."

Harry's pulling on my shirt. "Now. We're late."

Before I can turn to leave, Amy's at my shoulder, on tiptoes in her heels. She plants a sweet kiss on my cheek, my hand going around her waist, palm across her shoulders.

"I mean it, Hamish. Thank you."

"I get a kiss for being a decent man? How good to I have to be to get a shag?"

Harry's started walking away but hears it, laughing his ass off.

She pulls back and smacks my chest. "And there you are, back to being the lout. You have to ruin everything."

"Nae, Amy. Not everything. But I am who I am and I won't change for anyone. Remember that. Don't you dare let people like Davis for ye to change, either."

And with that, I join Harry, jogging toward the exit of the stadium, ready for the run back to Amherst College. I'll need the miles to burn off the lust she just triggered in me.

Worse? The deeper need.

Find your copy of *Shopping for a Highlander* now.

ACKNOWLEDGMENTS

When I decided, long ago in 2014 that Declan McCormick would have a Scottish cousin, and that Declan's incoming sister-in-law would be Hamish's person, I thought that I would have ongoing access to fly to Scotland and have some fun there.

And I did, in 2016 and 2018. Even got trapped in Edinburgh in 2018 by the superstorm that hit, shutting down much of Great Britain. (That's where the idea for *Fluffy* came to me).

I assumed I'd be able to immerse myself in the accent, see all the amazing sights, go to Glasgow and get a feel for how I wanted to depict Hamish, but alas, a virus changed all that.

So, instead, I decided to trap Hamish here.

I've also had to rework the plot for *Shopping for a Highlander*, which is the next book in Hamish and Amy's romance. But more about that in the future.

I am indebted to Kelly Allenby, my "Brit Checker," for her help in making me look significantly less foolish as an American trying to write a British character. Thank you for catching so many errors.

In addition, two Scottish readers, Karen Kerr and Lynne

Ferrie, read early versions of this book and gave me feedback to make Hamish's accent as close as possible to the real thing. Writing a book with a character whose accent I try to convey in the words themselves is hard (hello, Diana Gabaldon!). Hamish's inner thoughts are written in regular English, but his dialogue is not, and as a writer, I had to *stretch*.

To the point where I now think in Hamish's voice, ye ken, pet?

Every time I write a new book, I want to thank a bazillion people, from my regular beta readers (who know who they are), to my author friends who support and encourage me, to my Facebook group Laugh Your Way to Love, to my wonderful husband, Clark. My career has been interrupted by the pandemic (::waves in exhaustion at all the other people parenting during this::), but my imagination has not.

Neither has the goodwill of so many people.

As always, I'm so indebted to readers who like my books and love my characters. You make it all worthwhile.

OTHER BOOKS BY JULIA KENT

Shopping for a Billionaire: The Collection (Parts 1-5 in one bundle, 500 pages!)

- Shopping for a Billionaire 1
- Shopping for a Billionaire 2
- Shopping for a Billionaire 3
- Shopping for a Billionaire 4
- Christmas Shopping for a Billionaire

Shopping for a Billionaire's Fiancée
Shopping for a CEO
Shopping for a Billionaire's Wife
Shopping for a CEO's Fiancée
Shopping for an Heir
Shopping for a Billionaire's Honeymoon
Shopping for a CEO's Wife
Shopping for a Billionaire's Baby
Shopping for a CEO's Honeymoon
Shopping for a Baby's First Christmas
Shopping for a CEO's Baby
Shopping for a Yankee Swap

Shopping for a Turkey
    Shopping for a Highlander

Little Miss Perfect
    Fluffy
    Perky
    Feisty
    Hasty

In Your Dreams
    Her Billionaires
    It's Complicated
    Completely Complicated
    It's Always Complicated
    Eternally Complicated

Random Acts of Crazy
    Random Acts of Trust
    Random Acts of Fantasy
    Random Acts of Hope
    Randomly Acts of Yes
    Random Acts of Love
    Random Acts of LA
    Random Acts of Christmas
    Random Acts of Vegas
    Random Acts of New Year
    Random Acts of Baby

Maliciously Obedient
    Suspiciously Obedient
    Deliciously Obedient
    Christmasly Obedient

Our Options Have Changed (with Elisa Reed)
    Thank You For Holding (with Elisa Reed)

ABOUT THE AUTHOR

New York Times and *USA Today* bestselling author Julia Kent writes romantic comedy with an edge. Since 2013, she has sold more than 2 million books, with 5 *New York Times* bestsellers and more than 21 appearances on the *USA Today* bestseller list. Her books have been translated into French, German, and Italian, with more languages coming.

From billionaires to BBWs to new adult rock stars, Julia finds a sensual, goofy joy in every contemporary romance she writes. Unlike Shannon from Shopping for a Billionaire, she did not meet her husband after dropping her phone in a men's room toilet (and he isn't a billionaire).

She lives in New England with her husband and children in a household where everyone but Julia lacks the gene to change empty toilet paper rolls.

She loves to hear from her readers by email at jkentauthor@gmail.com, on Twitter @jkentauthor, on Facebook at https://www.facebook.com/jkentauthor . Visit her at http://jkentauthor.com